Deborah's Secret
Journal

Faith Kidz® is an imprint of
Cook Communications Ministries, Colorado Springs, CO 80918
Cook Communications, Paris, Ontario
Kingsway Communications, Eastbourne, England

First Printing, 2004
Printed in the United States
1 2 3 4 5 6 7 8 9 10 Printing/Year 08 07 06 05 04

Library of Congress Cataloging-in-Publication Data Applied For

Cover design: Marks & Whetstone
Cover illustration: Jeff Whitlock
Interior design: YaYe Design
Design Manager: Nancy L. Haskins

ISBN 0781440041

Secret Journals of Bible Time Kids
Volume 4

Deborah's Secret Journal

Equipping Kids for Life

An Imprint of Cook Communications Ministries
Colorado Springs, CO

A Faith Builder can be
found on page 132.

*To my dad,
whose trust in God is his greatest legacy.*

Contents

If Teardrops Were Flowers

Dear Journal,

I feel like I'm going to suffocate. On the outside I'm only twelve, but inside I feel older than the hills. I'm sick and tired of trying to be a mother to Salome.

I didn't feel this way three years ago, right after Mama died. Salome was tiny and pink back then, a newborn who didn't know the difference between a mother and a sister. All she needed was somebody who would keep her clean and dry, feed her, and hold her close. But that was then and this is now.

I should be out having fun with my friends, Ziva and Keryn, not tied to this house. I should not have a three-year-old sister who trails me everywhere and calls me "Mama." It's embarrassing! Salome is too young to understand that real mothers don't bake loaves of bread hard enough to pound nails. She doesn't know that real mothers don't have to wait until someone older can accompany them to the market. And she has no idea that most mothers know how to garden, weave, and sew. A hedgehog could sew better than I do!

As for gardening—forget it! I tried to show off by growing vegetables for Papa last spring, but everything except the onions died. And would somebody please tell me how to use 200 onions? Papa tried his best to console me. "That's okay, honey," he said. "You should have seen your mother's first garden. Pathetic!" We laughed hard. Somewhere in the middle, though, my laughter turned to tears.

I don't want Papa to worry about me. He has enough on his mind already, trying to keep up with his work. Our first year without Mama was tough. Last year was hard, too, but I found a few bright, happy moments to celebrate. Now, three years later, people still refer to me as "that brave daughter who stepped into Eritha's shoes." If only they knew my frustration!

Aunt Tara is my only hope of learning what I need to know in life. She and Mama were twins, and my breath catches in my throat whenever she arrives. Her smile is a reminder of everything I have lost.

Aunt Tara teaches me things without making me feel like I'm ignorant. (Does that make sense?) I used to pray that she would invite me to come live with her, but I finally stopped when she didn't ask. Besides, I could never leave Papa alone. Who would cook and clean for him? Who would talk to him in the evenings and listen to stories of his days as a young potter? "You girls keep me young," Papa likes to say. I wonder how young he felt this morning when he tripped over Salome's blocks on his way out the door.

Caring for Salome helps me feel like I'm doing something special for Mama. We play games by day and sing lullabies at night. And in between, I coax her into eating her vegetables—just like a real mother would do. Maybe that's why I feel such a mix of satisfaction and guilt. I'm glad to be raising my sister, but I'm also resentful that I have to be a mother to someone who's not even my child! When the resentfulness gets a hold of me, the guilt follows pretty quickly!

This morning Papa praised me for my patience. I wonder if God told him I needed to hear that today. "You're more than a sister," he said. "You're teaching her everything she needs to know to grow into a wonderful girl—like you. Mama would be very proud of you."

He's not around to see the times I feel like pulling my hair out. Salome can drive a person crazy, and she uses her voice like a secret weapon. She talks faster than anyone can listen, and she never, ever runs out of questions. Every question begins with "Why ...?" If I don't answer, that little girl has a way of melting my heart with those huge, expressive eyes. To be stared down by Salome is to gaze directly into my mother's face.

Papa stays busy. "Busyness keeps my mind pointing forward instead of back," he says. I wonder, though, if he ever just stops everything to spend time remembering. Housework and Salome keep my mind and hands busy, but honestly, I don't want to look forward all the time. I still want to remember life before Mama left us. Otherwise, I'm afraid I might forget her beautiful face.

I've prayed to see her in a dream, but so far that hasn't happened. I desperately want to remember everything about her: the crinkly smile lines at the outer corners of her eyes. Her sneak-up-from-behind hugs. The way her laughter bubbled up like a spring. Her middle-of-the-chin dimple. (I have the same dimple. Mama always called it our "family signature.")

Mama was my father's best cheerleader and encourager. When Papa started accepting custom orders for whole sets of dishes, word spread about the master potter from Jericho. Give Papa a lump of clay and he can make anything. (He once had an order for a kettle so heavy and huge, it took three men to move it.)

"Make me a new set of plates someday," Mama would hint, "a fancy dish set with wild pink roses running around the rims." She didn't live long enough to receive her new set of dishes, but she did capture Papa's heart for fifteen years.

I never smell a rose without thinking of Mama. I hear her laughter riding on the breeze, and sometimes, in those last dim moments before sleep, I imagine that she's sitting on the edge of my bed, singing to me. Mama's voice was pure and sweet, like the warbler that has adopted our sycamore fig tree out back.

Mama, why did you have to leave so soon? One life slipped away while another took its first breath. The midwife who helped deliver Salome hung her head in disbelief. She struggled to speak, but words would not come. When she could finally look me in the eyes, she whispered, "Your baby sister needs you. Be brave, child. God will help you."

She was right. God *has* helped me, but it hasn't been easy. Mama's friends like to remind me that life will get better, to just give it more time. I have no clue what that means. How could life without a mother ever end up better? When I'm forty, I will miss her as much as I do today.

Dear Journal,

Another mysterious bouquet arrived at our door this morning. The flowers never appear on the same day or at the same time, making it impossible to catch the person who delivers them. I told Papa that it might be Ori, the kind old man next door. He loved Mama's name—Eritha—and reminded her often that it meant "flower." Ori can identify every flower growing on the plains of Jericho. "Even the stinkweeds!" Mama would tease.

Papa thinks Midwife Mary is the one who might be leaving flowers at our door. She rarely passes our house anymore without asking about "baby" Salome. "She might feel responsible for your mother's passing," said Papa. "It wasn't her fault, but guilt has a way of torturing a person's soul."

I secretly wonder, though, if the pretty widow woman at the vegetable stand might be the one behind those bouquets. I think she has her eye on Papa. (He sums up my suspicion in one word: "Nonsense!") If I catch her leaving flowers, I'm going to hand them back and send her running!

If teardrops were flowers, I would have cried a sea of rosemary, purple kipodan, and yellow lilies by now. The pathway up to our door would be lined with bluebonnets and blooming aloe. And the house would be filled to the ceiling with pink roses. I don't cry as much anymore, thank God. Aunt Tara taught me to latch onto a favorite memory and hang on tight. That helps a lot.

Dear Journal,

A crescent moon stood guard over our house tonight. I lay on my bed, straining to hear the "whoo-hooo! whoo-hooo!" of our resident owl. Once I hear its familiar good-night, sleep comes easily. Mama used to tell me the night owl sat on a branch close to our house so it could eavesdrop on our bedtime stories.

Salome snuggled close and buried her cold toes in the bend at the back of my knees. I didn't dare move once she was comfortable, or she'd wake up. My sister talks in her sleep, and I have the best time interviewing her! I can ask her anything and she'll answer.

Mama used to say that Papa's snoring could wake the dead! I wish it could awaken her tonight. She would laugh and tell him to turn over and quit scrunching his chin too close to his chest.

GOOD NEWS! Papa has promised to give me another boxful of potsherds. The broken pottery pieces are fun for Salome. I am teaching her to draw shapes and numbers with a piece of charcoal. Salome is smart and curious about her world. Mama would be proud of her.

In Search of Wings

Dear Journal,

Mmm-mm! Our house smells like lavender, thanks to yesterday's mystery bouquet. I borrowed a sprig to hang on the corner post of Mikko's pen. That fat, lazy old goat stopped giving milk and now lives like a queen, demanding food and offering little in return. Maybe the flowers will sweeten both her pen and her disposition.

Salome has been trying to turn Mikko into a beast of burden, but Mikko is too smart for that. So Salome uses me, instead. "Deborah, carry me!" she says, crawling up on my back. "Take me to see Queen Mikko!"

This afternoon I hauled her around on my back until I felt like a swayback mule. It wore her out and now she's napping. She's also mumbling in her sleep again. I'm tempted to tickle her foot, which is hanging out the end of her blanket, but I'd much rather savor the peace and quiet!

I'm sipping grape juice as I write. Ori brings us a jarful of his specialty every year. Mama always thought Ori's grapes were the best. He would beam when she called the juice "heavenly nectar." I roll the sweet juice around in my mouth to coat my cheeks.

Mmm-mm. Mama, you would love this batch.

My list of chores is nagging at me, but first I'm determined to write in my journal. I never have time for writing when Salome is awake. I have to hide my journal in Mama's spice cabinet, where my sneaky sister cannot find it. Salome is too short to reach the shelf, and Papa never looks in there. (I don't think he'd know one spice from another even if they jumped off the shelf and introduced themselves.)

I didn't need a journal as much when Mama was around, but after her burial, Aunt Tara took me aside and suggested it. "Write down your thoughts, and your burdens will eventually grow wings." At the time, I thought that was a crazy thing to say, but now that I'm older, I understand.

Aunt Tara is the one who helped me through the dark days after Mama's passing. She doesn't offer advice often, but when she does speak up, I know it's something worth hearing. After all, she is Mama's flesh and blood. They played together as children and shared secrets late into the night. When I spend time with her, I feel connected to Mama. Sometimes we talk; other times we walk or do nothing at all.

Ever since she was a young woman, Aunt Tara has longed to have a baby. (I know it's true because Mama told me so.) The one time I asked my aunt about it, she answered softly, "God chose not to bless me with a child."

Aunt Tara journals every day, like me. It shows, too; her burdens seem to have grown wings and flown away. It shows in the warmth of her smile and the way she tries to fill in for Mama. She and Uncle Yavin stop for a visit whenever they come to Jericho.

My heartbeat changes to drum mode when I hear her squeal, "DEB-or-ah!" She races toward me with her dark, coarse hair flying behind her. "How are you?" When she speaks in that sugar-coated voice, it's like hearing Mama all over again. Aunt Tara and

Mama were the official family gabbers. Nobody dared enter the kitchen when they were together. They were big on talking and short on listening, like two hens clucking about their day.

Some people had trouble telling them apart, but not me. Mama had a dimple in her chin. Aunt Tara doesn't. And Mama could cook—boy, could she cook! She stirred, flipped, mixed, fried, and baked. Aunt Tara just stirred and talked nonstop.

Uncle Yavin is the opposite of his gabby wife. He's soft-spoken—more like Papa. Maybe that's why he and Papa get along so well. My uncle is three hairs shy of total baldness, but his eyebrows are so bushy, I could dust the furniture with them. Uncle Yavin studies what a person doesn't say as much as he listens to what they do say. The last time he visited our home, he stared Papa down and then whispered to me, "Your father needs a hobby—something to get him out of that dreary, dusty pottery shop. Doesn't he ever come up for air?"

"Only when he eats and sleeps," I said. Papa threw me a look so sharp, I could have sliced bread with it.

"Hiram, could I have a word with you?" Uncle Yavin asked. They stepped outside for a man-to-man talk. Aunt Tara kept Salome busy while I prepared dinner. Lucky for me, Papa and Uncle Yakin stood under the kitchen window, where I could hear everything. And I mean *everything*.

"Yes, I'll admit that I'm burying myself in my work," said Papa. "But Yavin, you have no idea what it feels like to lose someone like Eritha. She was my life! If not for Deborah and Salome, I would probably work the whole night through," Papa said.

Sometimes you do work all night, Papa. Remember the night I woke you in your shop, slumped over a dried-out lump of clay?

Uncle Yavin is a man who never intentionally hurts anyone. He steps around caterpillars and ants. He cups his hands over fluttering moths and releases them outside. "Work is admirable, but it's not enough, Hiram," he said softly. "You need rest—and I don't mean sleep, either."

"Work is good for the soul!" protested Papa.

My uncle wouldn't give up. "Listen, Hiram. You cannot go on like this forever. Look at your eyes! They're hollow. You've lost your charm, your fun-loving personality. True rest comes from God. When are you going to give him your cares and move on?"

At that very moment, an idea sailed through the kitchen window and struck me. *Papa needs a journal—a place to unload his worries.* I decided right there and then to talk to him after Uncle Yavin and Aunt Tara left for home.

Dear Journal,

Guess what? I talked to Papa about my journal.

"I'm glad it's helping you," he said.

"Wouldn't you like to keep a journal, too?" I asked him. "It's one way to get all your worries out of your head."

Papa isn't one who pretends. He wears his opinions on his tunic sleeve, so he didn't waste time laughing at my suggestion. "Tell me, Deborah, how many men do you know who keep a silly old journal?" He kissed my cheek and lifted my chin to make his point. "Thanks for worrying about me, though. I'm alright. Really, I am."

I've learned that you can't argue with a headstrong man. Papa has no idea what he's missing. I, for one, couldn't get through my day without my journal. I don't fume inside my head anymore. Instead, I write it all down. After a day of chasing after Salome, I deserve some comforting time alone, and that's what my secret journal has become—a comforting place to escape.

Dear Journal,

Salome didn't sleep long this afternoon. She had another nightmare; that same dream where a wolf chases her down and nips at her heels. It's a childish version of the nightmares I've been having since our mother died. Salome woke up rubbing her ankles. "Mean wolf!" she sobbed. "Look, he bited my foot, Mama!" I took down the jar of palm salve and pretended to rub it on her feet to soothe the imaginary bite marks. Then I chased off the wolf with my broom.

Papa popped his head into the room to investigate. "What's all the commotion about?" he said. "I felt the earth quake from all this noise."

"Mama scared the wolf away," said Salome, leaning her head against my shoulder.

"No, honey; *Deborah* scared the wolf away," said Papa. "Deborah, not Mama." He kissed Salome's forehead. "Hide the kiss so it won't fly away," he said affectionately.

Salome covered her mouth with her hand. "Mama," she whispered repeatedly to herself. I didn't have the heart to correct her again.

A Special Request

Dear Journal,

Papa's birthday will be here in a few days. Many Hebrews don't celebrate their birthdays. They think it brings too much attention to themselves and is like putting themselves on a pedestal or something. Mama thought that was a silly rule. "We aren't worshiping ourselves, just thanking God for giving us life, that's all."

If my mother were here, she'd bake Papa's favorite apple cake. She'd also buy him a gift at the marketplace—maybe a fancy tool for creating pretty edges around his clay pots. Or maybe she'd make him something herself. Papa collects decorative gadgets the way I collect bits of yarn and cloth to create dolls for Salome. Each of his tools has a special use. He even sharpened one skinny wooden stick to use as a writing instrument. While the clay is still soft, he autographs the bottom of his creations.

Papa has gotten very absentminded lately. He leaves his tools lying around, and half of his stuff is now missing. If Mama could see his workshop, she'd shake her head and call him rattled. "If your feet weren't attached to your body, you'd misplace them, too," she used to say.

Papa's pottery workshop is only a few steps from our house. I can visit him anytime I feel like it, but I'm not allowed in when he's talking business with customers. Sometimes I slip in there to sit beside him and just watch. I wish he'd let me use the tall stool—the one Mama liked to pull up close to his pottery wheel. Her stool is gathering dust and cobwebs in a corner. That's stupid. You'd think Papa would at least use it for a plant holder or something. I asked him if I could use it in the kitchen, but he said no. He treats that stool like it's made of pure gold.

I can still picture Mama perched there, her middle swollen by a growing baby. She's sitting close, watching my father's clay-crusted hands form the lip to a water pitcher. She doesn't interrupt him with words, but her presence speaks a language of its own. She loves this man—this childhood friend who won her heart when she was barely fifteen years old.

I only heard Mama interrupt his work once, when Papa was creating an anniversary bowl for Aunt Tara. "Could you add a design around the rim, Hiram?" she asked. "It would add such a pretty touch. Besides, you know how Tara loves your work." Her voice sounded like honey dripping from a spoon. How could Papa resist?

He pressed a small stick, sharpened to a point, into the soft clay, then pulled it back and pressed a second time in another direction. After working around the entire rim, he held the bowl up for us to inspect.

"Oh Hiram, it's lovely!" cried Mama.

I disagreed. "It looks like chicken scratches," I said.

He kicked me out of his shop for that remark. "Out! Out!" he said, trying to sound insulted. "You women are making me nervous."

Dear Journal,

Aunt Tara and Uncle Yavin stopped by our house today. I could hear them coming long before I saw them. Uncle Yavin's cart squeaked under the weight of wooden products he'd made for one of the merchants in town. He's one of the best wood artisans around, and like Papa, is sometimes so busy he has to turn customers away.

Aunt Tara remembered Papa's birthday. "If you want to buy him a gift, I'll go shopping with you," she said. She knows what a bad seamstress I am. If I attempted to make Papa a tunic, it would come out lopsided—a waste of good cloth. It's fun shopping with Aunt Tara. I love the sounds of the crowded marketplace, where merchants from faraway places display their wares several times a year. Everyone chatters at once in their thick accents. I like the clinging and clanging of money being exchanged and the musky stench of animals resting behind the market stalls. The only thing I don't like are the flies. Wherever food is displayed, flies show up, as if God gave them a map to the market!

"Maybe we could find your papa a new apron for his shop—one with a deep pocket to hold all his tools," Aunt Tara suggested.

I hoped she wouldn't feel let down. "Ummm ... well, I was hoping to ask Uncle Yavin for a special favor—something I can't buy at the market," I said.

"Your uncle's in a hurry this morning, Deborah, but we'll stop by on our way home. You can ask him then."

Salome overheard my conversation with Aunt Tara, especially the word "birthday." She roared into Papa's workshop singing, "Papady's birthday! Papady's birthday!"

I caught her by the back of her sash and spun her around. "Salome, your mouth is bigger than your brain. Can't you see that Papa is working?" Before she had a chance to run away, I scooped her up and hauled her kicking and screaming back to the house. "Mamaaaaa-aa!" wailed Salome. "I was just tellin' Papady 'bout his birthday!"

"Sh-hh, Salome! We want to surprise Papa on his special day. It's supposed to be our secret, okay?"

Salome pulled out of my reach and stomped off in the direction of Mikko's pen. Whenever my sister is mad, she heads straight for that smelly goat pen. She prefers the company of a goat behind a gate because the goat can't talk back. At least I can escape to my journal when I need to whine.

I ignored Salome's outburst but kept a close eye on her. I knew she'd call for me sooner or later, and she did. "I'm sleeping here with Mikko tonight! You don't like me anymore. Mikko likes me!" She pushed her chubby face through the fence rails. "And I'm not coming out!"

I like a good challenge, but I wasn't about to wade through goat dung to prove it. "Fine," I said. "Have it your way, Salome. Go ahead, sleep with the smelly ol' goat, but watch out for the wild beasts tonight. They like to nibble on chubby arms and legs."

You should have seen Salome fly out of that pen!

Dear Journal,

When my aunt and uncle returned, he unloaded a large goatskin bucket and carried it into the kitchen. Water slopped across the courtyard, making dark splash marks in the packed earth. "We thought you might be running low on water," said Aunt Tara. (How'd she know?) I felt like kicking up my heels and celebrating. *Hurray! I won't have to visit the city well today!* It's a major pain to wait in line with all those older women at the well. At my last visit, one of them stared me down and asked how old I was. I hate the age question. Just because I look younger than twelve doesn't mean they should assume I'm immature.

"Why doesn't your mother draw her own water?" she asked. "Seems odd to send a skinny lil' thing like you to do women's work."

I'm usually not fresh-mouthed, but this time I heard myself say, "It's not odd at all, because my mother is dead." A hush fell over the whole line, and the lady didn't say another word, not even an apology.

I watched Uncle Yavin refill our water container and grabbed his arm before he could leave. "Aunt Tara, could you entertain Salome for a couple of minutes?" I called out. "I need to ask Uncle Yavin a question."

Uncle Yavin was a busy man, and like Papa, he often accepted more work than he could handle. I picked at my fingernails and silently willed him to agree. *Please say yes! Oh please, please, please say yes!* "Uncle Yavin," I whispered, "Papa's birthday is only a few days away. I was wondering if you'd make him a gift for me." I searched his eyes for a reaction. "That is, if you have time," I added politely.

Uncle Yavin grinned—the response I was hoping to receive. "What did you have in mind, Deborah?"

"A box. A small wooden box with hinges, so Papa can keep track of his tools."

He tugged thoughtfully at the curly ends of his beard. "Hmmmm. A toolbox—in three days? Sure, I think I could manage that."

Should I ask him the rest? "Oh, but wait! There's more. I was wondering, could you maybe carve a rose on the lid? Oh, and the letter *E* in the middle of the rose?"

Uncle Yavin squinted his eyes. "*E* for Eritha. Nice! So what you really want is a wooden toolbox charading as a work of art?"

Mama's life had been a true work of art. I couldn't think of a better birthday gift for Papa than a toolbox to remind him of her. But was I asking too much of my uncle in such a short time?

"Consider it done," he said, pecking my cheek. "You're as thoughtful as the day is long, Deborah."

I flew at him with a hug. "Oh thank you! Thank you! But remember, it's a secret, Uncle Yavin. Promise you'll not slip and tell Papa?"

He patted his chest. "You have my word."

A Comforting Connection

Dear Journal,

Midway through the night, I awoke to the sound of my sister crying. "Ow! Owie-eee! Something *bited* my arm!" In the dull light of a waning oil lamp, I saw an angry red lump swelling in the crook of Salome's elbow. In the middle of the lump were two tiny marks—a fresh puncture wound.

Spider bite! Chills raced across my scalp. I only knew of two kinds of spiders—harmless and poisonous. Time would tell which kind had bitten Salome.

Salome clawed at her arm. "Make it go away!" she cried over and over.

Papa comforted her while I heated a pot of water. "Papady, it hurts! Make it stop hurting!"

I dipped a strip of clean linen in the hot water and then folded it into a neat rectangle, as I'd seen Mama do a few times. "Hold out your arm, Salome," I said. She squeezed her eyes shut and hummed extra-loud. You'd think I was preparing to torture her!

"Relax, Salome," said Papa. "Deborah is just trying to help you."

Bonnie Bruno

I pressed the warm compress against her swollen arm. "Hold it there for a few minutes. It'll help draw out the poison."

Salome looked like a forest animal caught in a trap. "Poison? I have *poison?*" she cried. "What's poison?"

"I think a hungry little spider might have nibbled on your arm," I explained. "It probably hitched a ride from Mikko's pen yesterday and thought, *What a yummy treat! She's sweet enough to eat!*"

"Deborah, you're scaring her," scolded Papa.

Salome winced. "Bad Mikko!" she cried. "Mikko let the spider get me." She leaned toward the doorway and repeated it louder, so Mikko would hear. "Bad, bad Mikko!"

Once again, I felt like a kid trying to fit into her mother's shoes. I could fold a compress, but I didn't know the first thing about handling an emergency—not really. Aunt Tara's words revisited me: *Write down your thoughts, and your burdens will eventually grow wings.* If that's really true, I have a lot of writing to do.

Dear Journal,

After our midnight excitement, I couldn't go back to sleep. What if the bite was poisonous? I'd heard stories of people losing their minds with fever or dying from an infected bite.

At the first hint of daybreak, I reached over to check my sister's arm. The red bump had swollen into a hot, oozing mound. "My owie hurts sooo-oo bad!" she said sleepily.

"Papa, wake up!" I whispered, shaking him hard. He had spread one of our spare bedrolls on the floor next to Salome's bed, where he'd eventually fallen asleep.

Papa laid his hand across Salome's arm and leaped out of bed. "Salome, wake up, honey. We need to get ready for a little trip."

I helped my sister slip her throbbing arm through the sleeve of her tunic. There wasn't time to braid her long, wavy hair, so I tucked it inside a scarf. "Keep your scarf on," I said, wrapping it snugly around her neck for warmth.

I filled a small pouch with bread and sweet figs. The journey was not long, thank God. I thought of asking Papa if I could go, too, but he needed me at home. A customer would be stopping to inspect the progress of his order. Papa was counting on me to show him the pottery pieces he had already completed.

Besides, I couldn't do anything more to help Salome. Uncle Yavin and Aunt Tara would know what to do. They'd found plenty of creepy critters nesting inside Uncle Yavin's stacks of wood. He'd quickly become their neighborhood's expert on spiders and snakes.

Salome didn't care whether he's an expert or not. She did not want to leave home without me. "I want to stay here with you, Mama!" she cried. Then she hung on my leg and wouldn't let go.

Mama. Would I ever get used to her calling me that?

"Aunt Tara and Uncle Yavin will take good care of you," I promised, smoothing her bangs away from her eyes. "Aunt Tara is the best cook in Jericho, and Uncle Yavin has lots of stories tucked away in his head."

Salome let out a long sigh. "But I like your stories better."

"Papa and I will come for you in just a couple of days. Your arm will be all better by then, and you can come home."

Her huge gray eyes welled with tears. "Promise?"

"I promise." I spoke the words as if I believed them, but my insides twisted with a combination of worry and hope. *Is this how a real mother feels?*

Papa hitched up our faithful donkey and spread a wool blanket across its back. Phew! Rudy smelled like a rug that needed a good shaking. Salome straddled Rudy and Papa climbed up behind her. "Keep an eye on my workshop," he told me. "I'll be home later this afternoon." I blew kisses to Salome as they rode off, and then I stood there until Rudy's silhouette faded into the sunrise. *Get well, baby sister,* I whispered.

Dear Journal,

It's so quiet with Salome gone, I can hear the crackle of palm fronds lifting and falling in the breeze. I've grown so used to her snoring, sleep-talking, and late-night questions, the house feels empty without her.

I'm fretting over that ugly, oozing spider bite. Did I do the right thing, applying a warm compress? Should I have applied ointment instead? *What would Mama have done?* I don't remember my mother ever flying into a panic, not even the time I caught my sleeve on fire. She had a natural sense about what to do in any situation, like a palace guard braced for an invader. I remember her little kit of emergency items—linen strips and a salve made from the juice of the date palm tree. Lucky for us, Jericho is known as "The City of Palms," so we never run out of ointment. Mama claimed that palm salve would remedy everything from chapped skin to the "aches and pains of chasing after ornery children."

After she died, I thought it might cure a broken heart, too. (It didn't.)

I inherited Mama's dimpled chin, but not her calm nature. I'm more like Papa, a run-in-circles type. In his hurry to seek help for Salome, he took off this morning without fueling our cooking stove. No problem; I'm hardly helpless! Papa stores dried-grass bundles in a bin near the stove. I tossed a fresh bundle on the embers at the base of the oven, and within seconds it burst into flames, sending waves of heat rippling through the house.

Now I have no more excuses. The fire is blazing. The house is quiet. Today I have to tackle my least—favorite household chore:

baking bread. I love a slice of warm buttered bread. (Who doesn't?) I'm just not crazy about the steps it takes to get me to that first bite, that's all. Flour flying in my face like dust. Sticky dough clinging to the spaces between my fingers. And the cleanup—that's the worst! I try to put off baking as long as possible.

Mama would have never run out of bread. She baked in big batches. She'd pull golden loaves from the oven and line them up on her kitchen shelf like trophies. "The more you bake, the more you have to give away."

Our flour bin is half-full—no grinding flour today. It's a tedious job, using a hand grinder that once belonged to my great-grandmother. I get chills whenever I think of all the other women whose hands gripped this very same tool. *Lord, did you watch my great-grandmother grinding flour for her bread? Did you know that I would be standing in for Mama someday, keeping a house, baking bread, and caring for Salome?*

I thought of them—women who had carried on the traditions of my family—and felt a comforting connection to my past. The regular bowl wouldn't do; I climbed on a stool to retrieve Mama's bulky wooden bowl from the top shelf. Dipping into the flour bin, I heard Mama's words: *It's just as easy to bake ten loaves as it is to bake three.* I measured salt and added three lumps of leaven to the mix. Leaven always turned my thoughts to my ancestors, whose preparations to flee Egyptian slavery didn't allow them time to wait for their dough to rise. So many thoughts, so many stories! I measured and stirred the ingredients into a big ball of glistening dough.

When I was a little girl, I'd beg Mama to give me my own little ball of dough. I'd pace back and forth, waiting for the dough to rise. "Good things take time," she'd remind me. When at last the dough was ready for shaping, I'd stretch and pat my little wad of dough into every shape imaginable. Mama could have tossed it into the trash, but she didn't want to hurt my feelings. She treated my dirty gray dough like a miniature masterpiece and laid it over the coals next to her big, beautiful loaves.

Today I laid my own beautiful big loaves—ten of them—over the glowing embers. *Good things do take time, Mama—it's true!*

A Blessing and a Curse

Dear Journal,

How I wish the wind would shift from east to west for once, instead of the other way around. I'd like those rich kids on the west side of Jericho to get a good whiff of my bread. They spend a few months in their winter mansions, as if life were one big vacation. (I've heard that those big houses have cisterns to collect rainwater, and some even have bathrooms where they can take care of their personal needs *indoors!*)

I'll bet most of those kids on the west side have never kneaded dough or washed dirty dishes. They probably have a maid who makes their beds for them. And when they're tired of wearing a certain outfit, they toss it in the trash and buy another. I bet their mothers don't even weave their own cloth like Mama did.

Someday I'll have my own life and my own children, and I'll teach my daughters to bake trophy bread like Mama's. I laugh aloud and suddenly realize that *hope* has visited my heart today. It feels good to think ahead. I wish every day were like this.

Hope also pulled me out of a slump and sent me into a cleaning frenzy this afternoon. I swept corners and rearranged furniture. Decluttering helps me unravel thoughts and works up a good sweat. I made another unexpected discovery today: Tucked in a dark corner under my bed, I found a missing necklace. It's the one Papa gave me when I turned twelve and the one that my grandmother gave to Mama on her twelfth birthday, too.

The day I lost my necklace was one of the darkest days since Mama's passing. Whenever Papa asked why I wasn't wearing it, my stomach would twist into tight knots. "I don't want it to get all gunked up when I work in the kitchen," I'd say. How could I possibly explain how careless I'd been with something so precious?

But enough about that—today was a day to celebrate! I slipped the thin gold chain around my neck and admired it in the afternoon light. Its tiny gold links shone as bright as ever. In fact, today it looked and felt brand-new.

Our central courtyard lets plenty of air in from the outside, so I pulled a chair out there and closed my eyes for a few minutes. Mama loved the style of our open-courtyard home. Built to let in light and cool morning breezes, it has become my favorite sitting area. Our kitchen and sleeping rooms surround the courtyard like the spokes of a wheel.

From my chair, I can see passersby and hear the sounds of Jericho waking up in the morning and settling down at night. On a chilly morning, I stoke the courtyard stove, and the entire house is toasty warm in a few minutes.

My all-time favorite room of the house is the upper room, though. I miss those times when we all used to sleep up there on hot nights. I was never quite tall enough to see over the retaining wall, so Papa would lift me on his shoulders to give me a good view of the city. Eastern Jericho—my side of town—looks prettiest at night, when lamps glow softly in windows and on courtyard tables. On a clear night, it looks like I could reach up and grab a fistful of glitter. If starlight were wishes, I'd grab a handful to tuck under my pillow tonight.

Salome is old enough to experience the rooftop. Maybe I'll introduce her to the glitter this summer. For now, though, I need to get her used to sleeping somewhere besides my bed. At three years old, she's much too clingy. (Besides, I could use a full night's sleep, which is impossible when Salome sticks her feet in my face.) Today I moved an extra bed out of our guestroom and set it up a few inches away from mine. I hope Salome will feel like a big girl when she returns home and finds her very own bed.

Dear Journal,

Whenever I feel overwhelmed by my duties as a substitute mother, I remember my friend Ziva, who lives nine houses away from me. I don't see her as often as I'd like, because she's saddled with lots of responsibilities. She has six—count 'em—*six* brothers and sisters! She is also the oldest daughter, like me. The role of oldest daughter carries both a blessing and a curse. I thank God that I have only one sibling to care for. If Mama had left me with five brothers and sisters, I'd never see the light of day!

I freshened up and changed into a clean tunic. Papa would be home from my aunt and uncle's house in a few hours. He never minds if I visit Ziva, as long as I let him know. When he's busy working in his shop, I usually leave a scarf hanging on his workshop door before I leave. It's our secret code. I hung the scarf on the hook in case he arrived home early today while I was gone.

I was startled to find a tall gentleman and a pretty, dark-eyed woman tapping on Papa's pottery shop door. They'd come to inspect the progress of a dish set that Papa was making for them. I welcomed them inside and pointed to a row of dishes spread out on a display table. "Papa said he'll complete the set in about four days," I told them.

Their eyes danced with delight and they whispered to each

other like excited children. "My wife has been longing for a pretty dish set for years," the man explained.

She held a small platter up near a window where she could admire its swirly edge. "The pattern is even lovelier than I imagined," she said. I thought she was going to cry.

I had a great idea. "Take your time. I'll be back in a flash," I promised. When I returned, they were closing the door behind them. "Please thank your father for us," said the woman. "His work is flawless. How proud you must be of him!"

"And thank you for your business," I said, handing her a small wrapped bundle. "It's fresh out of the oven—my mother's recipe."

I spent the rest of the afternoon with Ziva, catching up on old news. What a crazy household! Three younger sisters clamored for attention, interrupting our conversation and cartwheeling so close, their feet flew within inches of my face. And the noise— I'm surprised Mikko didn't hear it nine houses away and run for the open plains. How does Ziva stand it? How do her parents keep from losing their minds?

We didn't have much time, so we talked fast. Her mother tried to grant us some privacy and even took a break from her loom to entertain Ziva's sisters. But remember what I wrote earlier, about a blessing and a curse? That's Ziva. Her sisters love her dearly— she has a sore neck from all their hugs—but they're demanding and argumentative if they don't get their way.

Even though her responsibilities are great, Ziva is not a full-time mama as I've become. She isn't the chief cook and house-keeper, but helps her mother whenever she needs a set of extra hands. Life hasn't been a party, though; a serious leg injury left Ziva with a terrible limp. In the past three years, Ziva has worked hard to exercise and strengthen her leg.

"Everyone said I'd never walk right again. Guess I proved them wrong, huh?" Ziva has a stubborn streak, and this time it paid off.

Like Ziva, I, too, am a fighter. I'm fiercely protective of Salome and don't like it when people toss us that certain look—the one that suggests I'm not caring properly for her. They gawk and whisper, and a few have even trailed us around the market. How rude is that?

Papa raised me to be mannerly, but I have the hardest time turning off those stares! Know what I do? I stop dead in my tracks and just smile at them. Drives them crazy every time. I also run home and pour out my complaints here in my journal. It's my best-kept secret, the one safe place where I can say whatever I feel, anytime—night or day.

Dear Journal,

I hurried home from Ziva's to start dinner. Papa showed up a few minutes later, tired and hungry. The house smelled like fresh bread, and I waited for him to notice my lineup of loaves. *No response.* He commented on the sparkling-clean house, gave me an update on Salome—her arm is not quite as swollen now—and headed straight for his workshop. "Call me when dinner's ready," he said.

I sank into a deep pout. *I'll make him beg before I'll bake another loaf,* I silently fumed.

By the time Papa returned, I'd worked myself into frenzy. "Everything okay?" he asked.

"Uh-huh," I fibbed. Sometimes a girl has to pout to make a point—or so I thought.

He pulled up a stool to help me chop vegetables for our meal. Then he tried to humor me—another big mistake. He poked his little finger into my dimpled chin. "Has anyone ever told you how your chin twitches when you're upset?"

I'm sure steam was flying out my ears and nostrils. I answered by giving him the silent treatment.

"Would you like to tell me what's wrong?" he finally asked. Papa might not be quick about handing out compliments, but he does know how to spot a rotten mood.

"Nothing's wrong." I didn't dare look him in the eye. Eyes tell the truth. "No, that's not true," I finally admitted. I looked him square in the face. "I worked all day to surprise you, Papa, and you didn't even notice."

"I don't understand, honey," said Papa. "What was I supposed to notice?"

I might as well have been talking to Mikko. "The bread, Papa! You didn't notice the bread! Count them—I made ten loaves, just like—"

"—like Mama would have done? I do appreciate it, honey. You've stepped into a tough role, and I know that. I'm sorry I'm such an oaf about noticing details. Forgive me?"

He pulled a loaf of bread off the shelf. "Mmm-mm, it's still warm! Should I see how high it'll bounce?"

"I won't dignify that remark with a reply," I said, mimicking the way Mama used to tease him back.

Papa sliced a thick piece and then closed his eyes. He used to drive Mama nuts, giving her bread the official "Hiram Taste Test." "Fluffy. Moist, but not doughy. Light. Tasty. And wow—I didn't break any teeth this time!"

That was the best compliment I'd received in ages.

If This Vase Could Speak

Dear Journal,

You'd think I'd be dancing and singing, but I feel strangely lost without Salome tugging at my sleeve. I woke up every few minutes last night, partly because I miss my sister, but mostly because I was cold. I thought of her in her own little bed at Aunt Tara's. Was she homesick? Did she peek up at the moon tonight? When they tucked her in bed, did she teach them our special "Under the Moon" song?

Look at me—I'm pathetic! One day I complain because I'm tired of Salome trailing me around, and now I'm lying awake in the middle of the night, worried that she might be homesick. If she has one of her scary wolf dreams, will Aunt Tara know how to comfort her?

When dawn finally arrived, I treated myself to a morning of nothingness. Doing nothing is hard work! Today was my last day off before Salome comes home tomorrow. No more sleeping until the sun rises and no more quiet moments in the middle of the afternoon. Salome will latch onto me like a second skin. She'll probably bring home a whole new set of questions.

Bonnie Bruno

No sense sitting around killing time, I thought, especially on a bright, clear morning like today. I slipped over to Papa's workshop to let him know I would be taking a walk. It's a good thing I watched where I was going, or I'd have tripped over a pile of debris he'd left lying right in front of the entryway. My father is the most creative person I know, but he's blind to clutter. Mama used to help him organize his storage areas and was a pro at keeping his floor free of junk. "You can't sell beautiful pottery from a pigsty, Hiram," she'd remind him.

The steady hum of his potter's wheel was a familiar comfort. When I was little, Mama and I would sit quietly beside Papa, watching him turn balls of wet clay into works of art. Today I left him alone, though. A layer of curly scraps littered the floor under Papa's workbench, but I didn't dare poke around with a broom until he was finished for the day. I headed to a storage area instead—a little-used corner where dust-covered castoffs sat like weary soldiers atop a long, narrow table. I lifted each item carefully, dusting as I worked my way through the neglected wares.

There I found a vase—a remarkable creation with a delicate, curled lip and rounded sides. It was rough compared to Papa's other work, and it didn't have a pretty border. No flowers or vines. No delicate swirls. Nothing. Still, I liked it. It would make a perfect vase for our mystery bouquets—much nicer than the old stained container I'd borrowed from the shed. I coughed to get Papa's attention. "Papa, could I have this old vase?" I asked. "It looks like nobody ever came for it."

His shoulders slouched and the wheel came to an abrupt stop. "Put it back where you found it, Deborah."

"But it's perfect, Papa. I was thinking—"

"Please. Put it back." His jaw tightened while he waited for me to respond.

I placed the vase back on its shelf in the corner, but not before

I noticed a marking across its bottom: an H and an E entwined like two strands of ivy. Hiram and Eritha—Papa and Mama? *If this vase could speak, what would it say?*

Papa wiped his gritty hands on his apron. "I think you've dusted enough for one day, honey. Thank you."

"I'm going for a walk," I said quietly. "I just thought you'd want to know."

My path led past Ori's house, down the road past a stately row of palm trees. Ziva's older brother says that if you stand still near the base of the trees at night, you'll hear mice scurrying up and down the trunks and playing tag on the fronds.

Two women waved to me. A goatskin bottle hung from a wooden frame between them. They rocked the bottle back and forth, checking every so often to see whether their cream had thickened into butter. Watching them was like stepping back a few years, to watch Mama and Grandmother working together in the courtyard.

I continued on, paying no attention to how far I'd walked. My toe kicked something round and hard. Funny, I'd never noticed a pomegranate tree on our street before. Whoever invented pockets deserves an award; I stuffed two pomegranates in each pocket and turned around for the walk home. From that moment on, everything changed.

An unfamiliar row of houses stretched down a hillside, connected by a worn wall. My house isn't fancy like the mansions on the west side, but I'd never seen anything quite like the sight before me.

"Hello!" called a girl about my age. I returned her greeting and almost hurried by, but she sailed into the street and met me head-on. "My name's Anna. What's yours?" Anna's eyes sparkled like someone who had discovered a hidden gift. "Where do you live?"

"Down there," I said. "At least I think it's down there. I think I might be lost."

Bonnie Bruno

Anna shoved her hands into a faded blue tunic that looked like it had been patched one time too many. "Want to stay awhile?" she asked. "You can meet my family."

"No ... I mean, not today. I need to get home. Tomorrow's my papa's birthday, and I have to bake him a cake."

Anna's face dropped. "My mama won't turn me loose in the kitchen yet," she laughed. "I caught the last cake on fire! Can you believe that?"

Anna was my kind of girl! I liked her spunk. "Well, at least come and meet my mama," she said. Without waiting for an answer, she turned and led the way up a sloping courtyard into a tiny house.

It was hard not to stare. Anna's house was made of mud brick like mine, except hers looked ancient. Splotches of patched areas were starting to peel and flake. *One good rain and this place will collapse*, I thought. Thankfully, we don't get much rain in Jericho.

A strong musty smell permeated every corner of the main room. The odor was so heavy, I coughed to relieve my itching throat. Empty except for a long mat—probably used in place of a table— the room held only a couple of dilapidated chairs. Five sleeping mats had been rolled and stacked off to one side. Anna's house was noticeably dark, in spite of sunshine leaking through holes here and there.

A cheery woman with dancing blue eyes motioned me into a cooking area, where a scrawny goat lay on a heap of straw in the corner. "He looks like my goat Mikko," I said, "except Mikko is fat and sassy and spoiled rotten. She's old and doesn't give milk anymore."

"Not this one," laughed Anna's mama. "She doesn't have the luxury of refusing. She's our only source of milk."

Two sweaty little boys roared into the house, brushing past me as if they didn't notice me there. "Boys, where are your manners!"

scolded their mother.

"Sorry," they said in unison. Turning to Anna, they whispered loud enough for me to hear, "Who's *she?*"

"Deborah. She lives down the street. At least I think she lives down the street," laughed Anna. Her laugh reminded me of wind chimes. "So, how old are you? Eleven? Twelve?" Anna guessed.

"Twelve and a few months," I told her.

"Same here," she replied. "Sometimes I feel much older, though."

If only she knew how old I feel! "Me, too."

I liked Anna's easygoing style. From the looks of her house, she had every reason to complain, but didn't. It was the closest I'd stepped to poverty, and I felt strangely uncomfortable. I felt like apologizing for my new tunic.

I didn't want to rush off, but chores were waiting. I don't know what came over me, but I heard myself saying, "I'd better get going, or my mama will wonder where I've run off to." Speaking her name out loud—*Mama*—sounded as foreign as the chatter between marketplace merchants.

I shoved my hands in my pockets self-consciously. "Oh, wait, I almost forgot! I have pomegranates. Want some?"

It was the least I could give to my newfound friend.

Bonnie Bruno

Double-Knotted

Dear Journal,

Strange odors seeped up our street. It smelled like Ori must be experimenting in the kitchen again. Next to flowers, Ori's main interest centered on inventing new ways to prepare traditional foods. Mama used to admire his creative streak, but to me his habits are just bizarre.

My stomach protested hungrily. If I hurried, I'd have time to prepare dinner before Papa closed up shop for the day. I'd been skittering from place to place and hadn't even thought about cooking or cleaning today. In fact, I almost felt like a normal kid with a normal life today.

Papa met me at the door. "Don't worry about dinner. I've got you covered." He winked and motioned toward the table, which he had already set. Papa lit a candle and then blessed our food and our home. It felt like a normal mealtime—the kind we used to have.

Warm tears teased the corners of my eyes. Sad tears are one thing—I've spilled my share of those—but happy tears embarrass me. When Papa left the room, I wiped my eyes quickly on my sleeve.

Papa had prepared some kind of meat—lamb (I think) seasoned with (I'm not kidding) cinnamon and garlic. CINNAMON and GARLIC! Mama used to tease him about his lack of kitchen skills, but I figured she was exaggerating for laughs. *Oh, Mama, if you could only taste this stuff!* And there's more! Papa surprised me with dessert: fig pockets—tiny fruit—stuffed turnovers. They weren't quite like Mama's, but close. "You should open a bakery shop, Papa." Fig pockets are one of his specialties. They're easy to make and even Papa can't mess them up.

Talking with my papa was the sweetest dessert of all, though. I told him about my walk this afternoon, how I'd taken a wrong turn and ended up meeting a new friend. "You should have seen Anna's house, Papa. I've never been anyplace quite like it. It's dank and dark, and it leans to the left. The mud-brick walls have been patched so many times, even the patches are peeling off."

I felt like adding, *Patched and peeling like your heart, Papa.* My father is a master at hiding his wounds. He wears them like an invisible banner, known only by God, and he patches them by burying himself in his work. When Papa hunches over his tread wheel, he doesn't have time to think. At least that's how it looks to me.

"This is nice," I said quietly. "We don't usually sit around after dinner and talk. I sort of miss that, Papa. Tonight reminds me of way back when—" I couldn't finish the sentence.

Papa gathered me in his arms. When I stopped crying he whispered, "We've come a long way together, Deborah. We're going to be fine, honey—just fine."

Dear Journal,

Tonight I'm sleeping in the upper room. When I was younger, it felt kind of creepy up here by myself, but no more. I love the fresh air and canopy of stars. A full yellow moon is aiming its beams all over Jericho, highlighting the boundaries of our city like a charcoal sketch. I spotted Anna's house way down on the corner a while ago. Her windows looked pitch-black, as if nobody lives there—a peculiar sight in the middle of a neighborhood glowing with soft lamplight.

A strong breeze is blowing a nauseous combination of cooking odors and dirty stables our way. In a couple of months, this upper room won't reek with such offensive odors. Spring will arrive, with its perfumed breezes. I remember when Mama, Papa, and I would carry our chairs up here on the roof to breathe in the essence of hyacinths and roses.

Last spring, Papa and I let Salome view the city lights for the first time. She was too young to remember it now, but Papa held her up high, so she could peek over the restraining wall. We spent our evening reminiscing. "Mama adored the view up here," I recalled, "but she loved the rose-scented breeze even more."

Papa changed the subject, as if he were remembering the rose-patterned dishes he had planned to make for her someday. *Someday*. I detest that word! There ought to be a law against putting things off until someday. Plans change and seasons come and go. Who but God knows how many more springs or summers any of us have left?

I broke the uncomfortable silence between us. "I wish Mama were here to smell the rosy breeze."

But tonight was a different story. Spring's balmy evenings haven't yet arrived. I scooted deep inside my covers under a glittery ceiling of stars and thought of five things I refuse to put off until *someday*—things I can do any day.

1. Say I love you.
2. Try something brand-new.
3. Visit a friend.

Bonnie Bruno

4. Accept help.
5. Forgive.

The last is the hardest. Some people—like Midwife Mary—don't even know how I feel about them. She acts like I'm an imbecile who can't figure anything out on my own! I don't want her stopping by here with her advice anymore. *Lord, if I forgive her ignorance, do I have to adopt her as a friend?*

I saw a light show tonight—not one, but four falling stars! Did God loosen them from their grip of the universe and send them spinning across the heavens especially for me? Mama had a word for a falling star: *freefaller.* I wonder if God ever snatches a freefaller in mid-flight and sets it back in place again. Could he fill it with new glitter-light and attach it to its assigned home with a big double-knot?

The thought made me shiver. I tucked my journal under my mat and waited for sleep to visit me. *Refill me with glitter-light, Lord. Double-knot me as tight as you'd like.*

Dear Journal,

If anyone says God doesn't hear our thoughts, they're wrong, wrong, wrong! He heard my thoughts. He paid attention to my prayers. And wouldn't you know—he sent Midwife Mary to try my patience today.

Mary said she was on her way home from a birthing and couldn't bear to pass our house without saying hello. I fidgeted and made uncomfortable conversation. "How's baby Salome?" Mary asked for the umpteenth time. I didn't feel like going into details about the spider attack.

"Salome is now three years old," I corrected her. "Hardly a baby, but she's doing fine, thank you."

"Well, bless her heart." Mary craned her neck and peered over my shoulder to the rooms beyond. "So, is she napping?"

"No. I mean, I don't really know," I stammered. "She might be napping, for all I know." The more I talked, the more I confused this person who had helped deliver Salome into the world.

Mary raised her eyebrows. I knew what was coming next. "For all you know?" she repeated. She spoke slowly, drawing out each word as if she were speaking to a toddler. "Deborah, dear, is everything alright? I know it isn't easy—"

Papa poked his head around the corner just in time. *Thanks, Papa, you've saved the day!* "Papa," I called, trying to fake excitement, "look who's here!"

Papa and Mary swapped polite greetings before she asked him, "So, how is the baby doing, Hiram?"

Papa chuckled and threw me a secret wink. "We don't have a baby around here anymore, but we do have one rambunctious three-year-old—right, Deborah?"

"For sure! *Rambunctious* is putting it mildly."

"So, then, is she napping?" Mary asked him.

I snuck a cross-eyed look to Papa.

"I would imagine so," he said. "If the spider bite came from a poisonous spider, I imagine she's taking more naps than usual."

Mary's mouth flew open, exposing two gaps in her bottom row of teeth. (She reminds me of a human flytrap.) "Maybe I should take a look—"

Papa let her off the hook by explaining the whole story. "Salome's in good hands. She'll be home soon."

Sometimes it's fun to keep Mary guessing. I wish she'd ask how the rest of us are doing. I'd gladly tell her what it feels like to miss sleep over a feverish three-year-old, or to comfort Salome after one of her nightmares. I doubt whether she's interested in hearing any of my stories, though. All she cares about is "baby" Salome.

Mary looked satisfied with Papa's answer. She changed the

subject, from Salome to the troubling tax situation. "If the government keeps turning its head to those hooligans who collect taxes, we'll all end up so poor, we won't be able to feed and clothe our children."

Hooligans? Where? What, exactly, does a hooligan tax collector look like? I'm not sure I'd recognize one if he swung from a tree past my window. Midwife Mary needs drama the way the rest of us need food, water, and shelter.

The Birthday Box

Dear Journal,

The floor pressed cold and hard against my bare feet this morning, sending shivers up my bare legs. Arrows of light streamed in from three windows, meeting in the middle of the courtyard like interlocking fingers. As I neared the kitchen, I felt a welcome rush of warm air. *Good! Papa remembered to fuel the fire before heading to his workshop.* Our old scratched teapot bubbled away on the edge of the stove in the same spot where it has sat for most of my life. I poured myself a cup of steaming tea and laid several leftover fig pockets on the warm bricks to heat.

The old fellow next door—the one Mama admired for his knowledge of plants—was at it again. Ori's off-key singing trespassed into our courtyard every morning. Papa seems to like it, but it grates on my nerves. *Why does he insist on weeding his garden so early?* I grumped. Why can't he sleep in for once?

I thought of Mama and how she used to treasure her quiet moments first thing each day. "Oh no," she'd groan, half complaining and half laughing, "Ori's out there serenading his weeds again."

Papa's shop door was ajar. When Ori came up for air, I heard the familiar whir of the potter's wheel. Papa's work is solitary, but he likes it that way. I wonder what he thinks about during all those hours alone? Did he remember that today is his birthday?

I added a pinch of cinnamon to my tea and poured another cup for Papa. I've gotten good at slipping into his workshop without disturbing him. I left the plate of pastries and tea on a nearby table where he'd find them. No time to waste; I had work back in the kitchen, where I'd gathered supplies to bake Papa's birthday cake.

I remember memorizing the apple-nut cake recipe years ago, from watching Mama in the kitchen. Well, actually that's only half true. I did memorize the list of ingredients, but I never quite understood how much of each ingredient I should use. Mama never measured. She'd dump in a cup of this and a cup of that. Sometimes the cake was a success, and other times it flopped. The year she died, I couldn't bring myself to bake the apple cake on my own, so Aunt Tara helped. Now, three years later, I'm looking forward to the challenge.

I like to bake early, when a cool breeze swirls through the house. It's a good way to make all our neighbors envious, too. The cinnamony smell of my apple-walnut cake is enough to drive anyone into the street. *Maybe they'll praise my domestic skills for once, instead of whispering about "that poor young thing who's stuck raising her sister."*

I'd worked myself into a tizzy when a sweet voice rang out. "Deborah? Hello? Anybody home?"

Then a second voice, laughing. "We know you're in there. Either come out, or we're coming in for you!"

Ziva and Keryn! I practically flew to the front door to meet them. How long had it been since I'd seen my two closest friends—a week? Two weeks? "I've been on vacation," I said.

"Well, not a real vacation. Just time out from Salome." I told them all about her spider mishap.

"We're on our way to check on Grandma. Want to come with us?" asked Ziva. She dropped to one knee and pretended to beg.

Petite, with silver hair that shone like starlight, "Grandma Z"—Ziva was named after her—welcomed all of Ziva's friends as if they were family. I could tell I was one of her favorites, because she said she admired my curious mind. (I think what she really means is that I ask far too many questions.)

I would have gladly dropped everything and spent the morning with my friends, but duty called. "I hate to say no, but I can't break away today."

Ziva and Keryn protested, so I squished all my reasons into a neat little package—"There's too much going on: Papa's birthday, Salome's homecoming, and baking this cake before we leave for my aunt and uncle's place. Besides," I added, "in case you haven't noticed, I'm still in my nightclothes."

Keryn made a face. "One of these days we're going to have to kidnap you, Deborah."

Ziva nodded and shook her finger at me. "You've just about run out of excuses, missy."

"Be my guest; go ahead and kidnap me," I laughed. "Just remember, though, that wherever I go, Salome follows."

Ziva and Keryn groaned in unison. They understood what it meant to wear the title of Big Sister. I'm not sure they understand what it's like to have a clingy three-year-old calling me "Mama," though. My role as a substitute mother involves so much more than meets the eye.

Dear Journal,

My stomach surprised me by fluttering anxiously as we neared the turnoff to Aunt Tara and Uncle Yavin's street. Salome had only been gone a few days, but it has felt like months. Aunt Tara noticed our arrival and rushed outside to greet us. "Shh-hh!" she whispered. "Come on in. Salome is helping Yavin fix a broken chair."

I tiptoed up to Salome and wrapped my arms around her from behind. She frog-leaped into my embrace and covered my face with sloppy kisses. "Mama! Mama!"

I figured my sister would miss me, but I never realized how much. At that moment, I didn't care that she called me *Mama*, either.

Salome stuck to me like sap. The minute I sat, she bounced into my lap. "I missed you? Did you miss me?" she asked, holding out her arm for me to inspect. "I wanted to come home, but Aunt Tara said no, and then my spider bite went away, so now I get to go home and—"

I tapped her lips lightly with my index finger. "Come up for air, Salome. I missed you too." Cupping my hand over her ear, I whispered, "Wait'll you see the big surprise waiting for you at home."

"Is it a present?" She twirled in circles until she fell into a dizzy heap at my feet.

"Wait and see," I said again.

My inquisitive sister badgered me all the way home about her surprise. Was it big or little? Something to eat? Something to play with? Did I make it myself? She tore into the house first and headed straight for her new bed. Looping her chubby arms around my neck, she sang, "I'm a big girl now! I'm a big girl now!" Then she ran out back to tell Mikko her big news.

Life is simple when you're only three. All you need is a warm bed, food to fill your tummy, people to hug, and an old goat who'll listen to your secrets.

Aunt Tara and Uncle Yavin arrived later in the afternoon for Papa's birthday dinner and brought a special guest along for the celebration: Mama's cousin, Mathia, who had recently returned to Jericho after a long absence. She and Mama were inseparable as children. Mama nicknamed her "the good cousin," because she refused to pull pranks on people. Mama, on the other hand, was forever getting in trouble for practical jokes.

Papa's apple cake was a hit. The best part, though, was watching him open his birthday present. I thought his eyes were going to pop out.

Uncle Yavin had created the best-looking toolbox ever. He'd sanded the wooden lid and sides smooth, and the entire box shone from the special oil he'd rubbed into the grain. Papa ran his hands around the seams, admiring his brother-in-law's artistry. "It's much too handsome to be a toolbox, Yavin. You've outdone yourself."

"Thanks. It comes with a price, though: I don't want to hear any more excuses about lost tools," kidded Uncle Yavin.

Aunt Tara dropped a small wrapped package in the toolbox. "Here's a little something to get you started, Hiram."

"And here's a little something just because," said Mathia. She smoothed a stray curl and waited expectantly.

Papa has never liked the limelight. He'd rather sit in the back and watch somebody else receive a surprise. This time, though, there was no escape. We sat forward as he untied his package. "Hurry, Papady! I want to see your present!" cried Salome.

Papa glanced at Mathia. "I'm almost afraid to open anything from you," he teased. He opened her small, square package and sighed. "Where in the world—"

"It's a little something I picked up in Jerusalem."

"A new coin pouch! You're very thoughtful. Thank you, Mathia."

Papa shook the new leather pouch. "So, did you fill it with coins, too?"

Mathia punched his arm. "You're impossible! How Eritha put up with you I'll never understand!"

I swallowed a lump in my throat. Our kitchen table needed laughter. We hadn't laughed that hard in a long while.

Papa opened Aunt Tara's package next and found a small wood-handled tool, curved at one end like a half moon. "It's for edging pottery that needs an extra-special design," explained Aunt Tara. "The merchant told me you can use it to create all kinds of interesting patterns—"

"Like tiny roses?" I asked.

Aunt Tara knew exactly what I meant and tossed me a wink. "Yes, like tiny roses around the rim of a plate."

I thought about Uncle Yavin's comment: *No more excuses. I have my own share of excuses, too—lots of them. My uncle says that an excuse can take root and wrap itself around you, like ivy crawling around a tree. Sometimes it feels like that invisible ivy is wrapped around my house, trapping me inside. It's easier to stay home than put up with the stares and comments of snoopy older women at the market or community well. Lord, help me to hold my head up high. I am doing the best I can.*

Up a Tree

Dear Journal,

I tucked my little sister in bed so I'd have time alone to write in my journal. Would she leave me alone? No. Did she like having her very own bed? Yes—for about five minutes. Then she wriggled out of her bed and burrowed deep under the covers of mine, where she thought I couldn't reach her.

I lay next to her until she fell asleep from sheer exhaustion. (Wouldn't you be exhausted after asking 300 questions in a row? Salome has a need to know everything: Why did God give us eyelashes? When will my feet grow as big as yours? Where does the wind go after it leaves Jericho? Why don't grownups play skipping games anymore?)

Once sleep overtook her, I pulled a bed switch: I'm now sprawled across her "big-girl bed" while she sleeps in mine.

Aunt Tara and Uncle Yavin left early to take Mathia home. It's going to be fun having Mama's favorite cousin living nearby. Maybe she'll tell me stories about their childhood that I haven't heard before. Mama called Mathia her "cousin who couldn't sit still."

Aunt Tara planted a big smoochy goodbye kiss on my cheek—the kind that sounds like a suckling piglet—and promised to visit us again soon when they could stay longer. "If you make any more delicious cakes like the one we shared tonight, Yavin is going to send me back for baking lessons!"

I don't like to brag, but I do think my cooking has improved. I once tried to cook a stuffed cabbage—a very big, stuffed thing with spicy meat and vegetables. It was so bad, even Mikko wouldn't go near it. Papa has referred to it a few times since as "Deborah's cabbage experiment." He is much too polite.

I hope to visit Anna again tomorrow. Papa says he's too busy to keep an eye on Salome for me, so I'll have to take her with me. I hope she doesn't say anything rude about their house. Three-year-olds don't usually think before they open their mouths.

Dear Journal,

I awoke to ten tiny toes digging into my ribcage. There's no escaping Salome when she's cold. I'm going to have to think of a way to get her to stay in her big-girl bed from now on. She clings to me like a stubborn wart.

I slipped out of bed and stuffed my pillow under the blanket where my body should be. A sweet, familiar scent tugged at me, so I tracked it down. It led me to the kitchen table, where a huge fresh bouquet of wild roses and greenery brightened the room. I leaned in close to get a good whiff. *Mama would tuck a rose behind her ear like this.* I broke off a small pink rose and did the same. Then I spooned fresh berries into a clean dish, laid a slice of warm cinnamon bread on top, and headed over to Papa's shop.

"Papa, where'd you find the flowers?" I asked.

"In the usual spot, right there on the front step," he said, rubbing his sticky hands on a cloth. He laughed at my puzzled expression. "You're our official family detective, Deborah. Sooner or later, I'm convinced that you'll unravel the mystery."

"Well, I hope I unravel it before it unravels me. It's driving me nuts!"

I'm glad Salome is back. As much as I gripe, our house has felt empty without her. This morning I decided that housework could wait. Salome and I need to build new memories together. "I want my new friend Anna to meet you," I said, pulling her hair back in a long, thick braid. "Anna has lots of brothers and sisters, too. Maybe you'll make a new friend today."

We stopped by Papa's shop to let him know where we were headed. "Anna's house isn't far—in fact, I spotted it from our rooftop the other night. We'll be back soon," I promised.

"Stay with Deborah," Papa cautioned Salome. His hands and wrists were gray from a layer of gunky clay, so he didn't try to hug us. When we passed his window, he blew us a kiss.

Salome poked along the edge of the road, stooping to pick up sticks and pebbles for her growing collection. A donkey waddled by, wearing saddlebags bulging with fresh produce for the public market. Its ruddy-faced rider nodded politely and smiled at Salome's enthusiasm for rock-collecting.

Salome didn't understand his friendly gesture. "Don't let him take my rocks!" she hissed. "They're mine!" I assured her that he did not look like a rock thief.

A steamy mist rose as sunshine played with the cool surface of the street. Salome broke free of my hand and raced ahead, where she'd spotted a shiny rock to add to her collection. She grunted and hoisted the rock up with both hands. "Deb'rah, will you keep it for me?"

"Sorry, my pockets aren't that big."

She pursed her lips and then let them drop into an ugly frown. "I can't carry it. It's too heavy!"

I've learned to ignore Salome's tantrums. She was still grumping at me when Anna spotted us. "Oh, good! I'm so glad to see you. Think you could help me with something?" We followed a shortcut down to her house and slipped around back. "Look!" she said, pointing frantically up a tree. "My brother's stuck."

Dear Journal,

I'm exhausted, just thinking about the rest of my day. Anna's brother is a handful! I peered up the tree and finally spotted him way at the top.

"Way up high!" cheered Salome.

"I'm supposed to be babysitting while my mother's at the market," said Anna. "Do you hear that, Nathan?" she shouted up the tree. "Like it or not, I'm *babysitting* you." She turned up the volume. "If you don't come down from there this instant, you're going to be in SO MUCH TROUBLE!"

Five-year-old Nathan straddled a high, thick branch, daring Anna to climb up after him. "Girls don't know how to climb. Girls are stupid, 'specially sister-girls," he mocked.

I tugged at Anna's sleeve. "Guys have bottomless stomachs, true? Do you think we could bribe him with a snack?"

"I can help," whispered Salome. She shaded her eyes and studied the stubborn kid up the tree. "How come you don't listen?" she asked him. "You're s'posed to listen."

"Because he's a boy," mumbled Anna, "and he thinks he's king of Jericho."

"Do not!" snapped Nathan. "I'm king of the *whole world.*"

"Kings don't look like you. And kings don't climb trees." Salome shot him a smug look and waited for his reply.

Nathan climbed higher. Salome shrieked, "You're gonna fall! You're gonna fall and break your head!"

I had an idea. "Salome, why don't you sit right here at the bottom of the tree. Keep talking to Nathan, okay? Tell him about your rock collection. Boys like rocks. I bet you have more rocks than anyone on our street."

Salome stretched her neck way back and waved to the scruffy kid at the top of the tree. "See? I have lots of rocks. Sticks, too. Do you like them?"

Nathan grunted.

Salome was a tireless talker. "I have a goat, too. You can't see her. She's at my house."

Anna and I made a beeline for the house. The kitchen was as dark and dreary as ever—nothing at all like the sunny kitchen at my house. I helped her slice two chunks of bread from a fresh loaf. "Nathan loves this stuff," she said, spreading one slice with amber honey. We topped the bread with thin slices of apple.

It looked tasty. "What do you call it?" I asked.

"I call it disgusting," said Anna, "but Nathan likes it."

"I'm glad I don't have any brothers," I said. "Salome is about all I can handle."

Sunlight blinded our eyes when we stepped back outside.

"Here, Nathan. I brought you—" Anna's sentence ended with a gasp.

Nathan and Salome were gone!

Bonnie Bruno

A Cheap Imitation

Dear Journal,

I thought my heart was going to stop. How could two kids disappear so quickly?

Salome's rocks lay scattered at the base of the tree, as if they'd been dumped or tossed. My sister was adventurous, but I doubted whether she'd be able to muster up the courage to wander too far.

"Nathan!" screamed Anna. "Get back here this minute or you're going to be in BIG TROUBLE!"

"They're just hiding from us," she said. "It's Nathan's favorite game. They must be around here somewhere."

We circled the house several times, calling their names and bribing them with promises we'd never be able to keep. And we threatened them with punishments that would drive even the most rebellious kids out of hiding.

Silence.

My throat tightened around my sister's name. "Salome! This isn't funny! You'd better come out—NOW!" We called their names until our throats hurt, gulping huge helpings of air in between pleas.

Bonnie Bruno

Several minutes later, we hadn't found either child. Anna shouted to nearby neighbors, who dropped everything to join our search. Our cries bounced off houses and echoed up the street. "Salome! Nathan! Where are you?"

I didn't dare speak what my heart was suspecting. *Had someone snatched Salome and Nathan while Anna and I were inside the house those few minutes?* I'd heard stories of kidnappings, but surely not here in Jericho! That kind of thing happened only in other places, not in my very own hometown, didn't it?

I thought of Papa back home at his potter's tread wheel, unaware of what was happening at the opposite end of his street. Panic seized me, and I raced toward home. Papa would know what to do. Anna tore up the street with me, and neither of us stopped until we reached the door to Papa's workshop. It was open, but for once I didn't care whether he was meeting with customers or not. We burst into the room, and I poured out our story.

"They're gone, Papa! We've looked everywhere! They're gone!"

I expected my father to race out the door in a panic and organize a huge search. Instead, he sat there with a big, silly grin as if he hadn't heard a single word. He nodded his head to the side, like someone trying to shake water out of his ear.

"Papa, this is serious! Salome and Nathan are missing! We've looked everywhere and—"

"Nathan? You mean the little freckle-faced boy up the street?" he asked, tipping his head to the right again.

"Yes! That's my brother! Have you seen him?" asked Anna.

Papa gestured with his thumb toward the back of the store, and my eyes followed his lead. There I noticed two sets of eyes peeking over a shelf way back in the corner. A pair of giggling voices rang out. "SURPRISE!"

My relief quickly turned to anger. "Salome! Where have you been?" I jerked her roughly out of her hiding place. "I've been worried sick. I told you to wait in Anna's yard, did I not?" My voice hung in the air like an ancient echo. *Listen to me. I sound just like a real mother.*

Salome wouldn't look at me. "I missed Papady," she said quietly. She pointed to his pottery wheel. "Look—he's making a dish!" I hated when she tried to change the subject like that.

Anna grabbed her brother's hand and led him outside for a good scolding. "Wait'll I tell Mama and Papa how you wandered off by yourself!" she threatened him. "You're in big trouble now, Buster!"

I didn't have the strength to yell any more at Salome. I'd already spent my energy in those few panic-stricken moments. Now that I'd found my sister, I aimed my anxiety toward God. *I'm only twelve—too young for this kind of stress, Lord! If Mama had been here today, Anna wouldn't have gotten lost. She would have watched her better. Salome deserves a real mother, not a cheap imitation like me. And I deserve a mom, too.*

Papa reminded me that I should never-ever-no-matter-what let Salome out of my sight. No fair! Why didn't he also lecture Salome on how she should listen to me and not wander off? If she had stayed under that tree like I told her to, this wouldn't have happened. It's as much her fault as it is mine!

I'm tired of getting blamed for everything my little sister does or doesn't do. The more Papa lectured, the more irresponsible I felt. "Look at me, Papa," I grumbled. "I'm too young to be a mother. I'm a sister, not Salome's mama! I'm not even half a mother. No matter how hard I try, I will never be anything but a sister to her."

I closed the door behind me and left them both in the shop. *If Salome is old enough to disobey and run off, then she's old enough to apologize, too!* I thought. Until she crawled to me with a "sorry," I would give her the silent treatment and see how she liked it.

Dear Journal,

Salome didn't apologize. She didn't come to me with a hug or anything. A few minutes later, she acted like she'd forgotten all about her runaway stunt. But when she turned those pale gray eyes on me, I saw my mother's face all over again. My heart softened, as usual.

Had I been expecting too much from a three-year-old? My sister didn't see anything wrong with tearing up the street and hiding in Papa's shop. To her it was just a fun game of hide-and-seek. She and Nathan followed their feet and didn't think about how worried the rest of us would be. *Was I ever that carefree, Lord?*

Papa and I had a long talk later, while Salome was napping. "Listen Deborah, I've been thinking about what you said, and you're right. I don't expect you to be Salome's mother. You deserve some relief—a day off with your friends now and then." He lifted my chin and kissed my nose the way he used to when I was younger. "How about tomorrow? Just let me know where you're going and when you'll be home. I'll keep an eye on Salome."

His words were more soothing than the finest palm salve, but I couldn't control a giggle that was building up inside me. I thought, *Papa has no idea what he's in for!* I sure wasn't going to warn him, either. Better to let him experience it himself. Salome would drive him batty.

Dear Journal,

Tonight I wanted to sleep in the upper room, but Papa wouldn't hear of it. I asked why and he rattled off a list of excuses: Salome might try to climb over the wall and fall to her death. If she has one of her wolf nightmares, her cries will bother our neighbors. She just got home; she needs to get used to her new bed downstairs. His list wrapped around Salome like a protective armor.

That's okay; I hadn't planned to take Salome upstairs, anyway. (Who can enjoy the starry sky with a three-year-old jabbering nonstop?) So I agreed with Papa. The rooftop wasn't a safe place for kids her age. I'd wait and sneak up there after I was sure she'd fallen asleep. After all, didn't he object to Salome sleeping up there? His list of reasons applied to her, not me.

My plan worked. Salome's big runaway adventure had left her exhausted. I tucked the blankets in snugly around her and waited until her breathing slipped into a slow, measured rhythm. Then I headed upstairs to my starry retreat. If she awoke in the night, I'd be able to hear her in the room directly below.

Fresh air and starlight have a magical way of easing me into sleep when I least expect it. I curled up in a ball, pulling my covers up around my chin. *Dawn will awaken me before Salome ever knows I'm gone.*

Beyond Repair

Dear Journal,

Dawn didn't awaken me, but Papa did. "Deborah, wake up! Do you have any idea where your sister is?"

I bolted out of bed and ran downstairs, where I discovered Salome's empty bed. *Oh no, not again!* Like a detective, I ran my hands over her bedding. "It's cold," I whispered. My stomach lurched, partly because Papa had caught me sleeping upstairs and partly because I was worried about Salome's safety.

A trail of cake crumbs put my mind at ease. Salome's raging appetite must have carried her to the kitchen for a middle-of-the-night snack. I followed the crumbs from the kitchen to a corner near the brick oven, where she'd curled up in a ball and was sleeping soundly inside her cozy blanket-cocoon. "Well, at least she didn't fall over the wall upstairs," I joked.

Papa was not amused. "You ought to be thanking God that she didn't wander right out that front door into the heart of Jericho!" he snapped. "Deborah, I need to know I can count on you. I shouldn't have to check up on you. I can't spend my time worrying about whether Salome is wandering around in the middle of the night."

Bonnie Bruno

It takes a lot to upset Papa. He was angrier than I'd seen him in a long time. "I'm sorry, Papa. I thought sure Salome would sleep all night. I planned to spend the night upstairs and then come down early this morning before she ever woke up."

"I trusted you. You chose to disobey. I'm disappointed that you didn't take me seriously." I felt lower than an earthworm. Papa's words hit their mark. I would much rather get a million scoldings than to hear that he's disappointed in me. Disappointment drops a gray, gloomy fog over my day.

"It won't happen again," I promised.

Papa shook his head and walked off mumbling. "I'm going to work," he said.

From the way he acted, you'd think I'd murdered someone.

"But Papa, remember how you promised to keep an eye on Salome today? I was planning to visit Anna. Is that still okay?"

He nodded on the way out the door. "Don't worry about us. We'll be fine," he said.

Papa, you have no idea what you're in for! I thought. Salome has the energy of three adults and can wear anyone down in a hurry. *By day's end, you're going to appreciate me a lot more than you do this morning!*

Dear Journal,

Anna was surprised to see me again so soon. "What kind of trouble do you think we could stir up today?" she kidded. "I thought my parents were never going to stop talking about Nathan's great escape."

I told her about my latest fiasco—how a simple night upstairs had turned sour.

"I don't get it. Why was that your fault?" she asked. "I'd be upset if my parents expected me to watch Nathan twenty-four hours a day."

I'd been thinking lately about how to open up more with Anna. If we were going to become close friends, I wanted her to understand more about me. I'd even rehearsed what I would say to her: *My mom's dead, and my dad's busy making pottery to put food on our table and clothes on our backs.* No, that sounded too harsh. How about: *My sister looks up to me like a mom, and my dad depends on me to watch her.* Nope. That wouldn't work, either. Maybe I'd just tell her the truth; that Mama died bringing my sister into the world.

"Hey, Deborah?" Anna snapped her fingers in front of my face. "State your name, birthplace, and favorite food. I need to know it's really you and not an imposter."

Anna knew how to make me laugh. "I'm free for most of the day. How about you?" I glanced over at her mother, who was hanging wet clothes over a sunny rack outside.

"Your mom must have a shorter list of chores than mine," said Anna. "I have to clean my room first. Mama's afraid it's going to attract a den of snakes if I don't do something quick."

I gave her an offer she couldn't refuse. "How 'bout if I help you? It'll go fast if we work together." I didn't mind helping with somebody else's chores. It's more fun cleaning a friend's room than my own.

"You're very strange, you know," said Anna. "I've never met anyone who likes to clean up other people's messes."

I followed her into the house. "Come on in, but watch where you step. My brothers aren't very good at picking up after themselves. I guess they take after me." We stepped over sandals and toys, through a room lit only by pale morning light. Darkness hugged the corners, creating gray, gloomy shadows. *Papa says oil is expensive nowadays.* Maybe her parents are rationing theirs.

A moldy scent stung my nose. Anna led me to a tiny room at the back of her house. "Well, this is it—my little corner of the world," said Anna. "It's where I escape when I want peace and quiet." Like the rest of the house, Anna's bedroom walls were marred and deeply chipped, as if someone had used her room for target practice. I tried not to stare at the flaws.

"It's not fancy, but it's still my own space, right?" Anna's room was so dim, it strained my eyes. I asked if she wanted me to help her light a lamp. She blushed. "Oh, we don't use lamps around here anymore. Oil has gotten too expensive, and even if we could afford the oil, both our lamps broken beyond repair." *That explains her darkened windows the other night.* "Until we catch up on our tax bill, Papa says we're going to have to do without certain luxuries.

Luxuries? I couldn't imagine getting along without light! "Well, my dad gets up so early, he'd trip over his own two feet if we didn't leave a lamp on."

"You're lucky to have a room of your own. I have to share mine with Salome," I said. "Trust me, Anna. A three-year-old and a twelve-year-old make verrr-ry strange roommates."

"Oh, your sister isn't so bad," said Anna. "She's sweet and testy, all rolled into one. I bet your mom was furious at her for running off yesterday, though."

I didn't want to lie, but the truth takes longer to explain. I barely knew Anna, but she was already beginning to feel like an old friend. Even so, I changed the subject. "Speaking of kids, did you know that a huge family used to live here in this house?"

"I know," she said. "They used to be our neighbors over in west Jericho, but that was a long, long time ago. When we heard they were leaving Jericho for good, they offered us their home. For the first time, we had a place of our own."

"You lived over *there*—in that fancy neighborhood?" I couldn't imagine Anna living in one of those fancy winter vacation villas. Most of the people there were only part-time residents of Jericho. They'd swoop into town and dump their money at the market, which pleased local vendors. Nobody knew them very well, though, because their children didn't mingle with the likes of us on the east side of town.

"Why would you want to leave a beautiful home over there—" My face flushed with embarrassment. Who was I to decide which neighborhood suited Anna's family? Did a fancy house make a person more likeable? Hardly! An awkward wall sprang up between us.

Anna shrugged at my shocked reaction. "Now, don't go getting all huffy," she said. "We lived in west Jericho, but trust me, Deborah—it wasn't a life of luxury. My parents worked for one of the homeowners there. Mama was a housekeeper and my father took care of the grounds."

"The grounds?" I'd never heard that term before.

"You know—the huge formal gardens. Papa has a reputation as one of the best gardeners around. He can't help himself; it's part of his heritage, I think. His father and grandfather could somehow coax a flower to bloom anywhere—even in dry, sandy soil.

Anna's mom stuck her head in the room to add her two shekels' worth. "We're still waiting for him to find the time to plant something around here," she said. "I'll bet our beautiful plants in the hills withered and died after we moved here. Those people depended on us for cleaning, planting, watering, weeding—everything. After years of working as someone else's servants, it's a blessing to own our very own home."

She talked about her house as if she were blind. Didn't anyone but me notice the crumbly old walls and tilted floors? How could anyone act so happy in a house that looked as though it might fall in on them any minute? I'd even seen people elbow each other and gawk at Anna's shabby house as they passed by.

Lord, is it really possible to find beauty where others see only ugliness?

All the Weak Places

Dear Journal,

I helped Anna sweep and organize her messy room. The swoosh of the broom pulled me into my own thoughts, and Anna noticed my quiet mood. "What's going on in there?" she asked, playfully tapping the top of my head with her knuckles.

"Oh, nothing. I was just wondering how long you've been managing without a lamp. But that's really not my business." *Why can't I learn to keep my mouth shut?*

"I'd be the first to light a lamp if we had one that worked, Deborah. That one over there is older than the city wall—sort of a family heirloom. It belonged to my great-grandfather, who dabbled in pottery-making. It has a slow leak and isn't safe to use, according to Papa."

I asked about the other lamp—the one I'd noticed on a stand in the front room. "Well, that's a long story," she chuckled. "Let's just say it's beyond repair, thanks to my grabby brother." Anna threw up her hands like it was no big deal. "But who's complaining? I just pray for moonlight and try not to stumble."

We worked fast together, rearranging clutter and assigning each item to its rightful place in Anna's room. "Can I adopt you as my twin sister?" she joked.

"No, but you can come over to my house sometime. Maybe we could plan a sleepover. Think about it."

I hurried home to fix dinner and discovered Mathia bustling around my kitchen like she owned the place. "Mathia! What are you doing here? How long can you stay?"

Mathia wiped her hands on a rag and pulled me into a tight hug. She smelled like violets. "Ever since my return to Jericho, I've thought about your family. Your mother helped me through a lot of tough times when I was young, Deborah. I figured the least I could do is to help your family once in a while." Mathia studied my face, as if she could intercept my thoughts. "You don't mind, do you? I mean, I'm not saying you need anybody's help, Deborah. I just thought—"

"No, no, it's fine, Mathia! Really, I'm happy to see you." I lifted the lid on a bubbling pot. "In fact, I was secretly hoping you'd visit us sometime. Mama used to rave about your cooking. She called you a cooking genius. Besides, I've missed you."

Mathia beamed. "Well, now that we're practically neighbors, I'm hoping we can spend more time together."

"Maybe you could share some family recipes with me," I said. "I get tired of making the same old thing." I swore her to secrecy and then told her about the meal Papa had cooked for me recently. "He spiced the meat with garlic and cinnamon, Mathia! Can you imagine? GARLIC AND CINNAMON!"

Mathia laughed so hard, she gasped for air. "Your mother was right when she referred to your papa as the quiet, creative type. Garlic and cinnamon-spiced meat is definitely creative!"

Salome bounded into the house, followed by Papa. "What timing! We were just talking about you, Hiram," laughed Mathia.

I stretched up to kiss my father hello. "Papa, did I mention that I was going to hire Mathia as our chef? Whatever she's cooking smells smell great!"

"I'm hungry!" sang Salome. "Do I have to eat the green stuff?"

"Vegetables," said Papa. "The green stuff is called vegetables, Salome."

After dinner, I chased Mathia out of the kitchen. "Go put your feet up and relax. You've done enough already."

Later on, I kept Salome busy drawing charcoal pictures on shards of pottery. Papa's scrap bin provided an endless supply of craft ideas. Salome loved discovering unusual shapes among the scraps. She'd outline them and add charcoal features to resemble a favorite animal. "Look, Deborah, this one is Mikko!"

Papa and Mathia sat across the room from us, sipping tea and catching up on family news. While they talked, Mathia sifted through a box of Mama's belongings—ribbons, embroidered linens, and other handmade items we'd set aside to share with Salome when she's older. Mathia didn't tiptoe around the subject of Mama, like others we knew. It was a comfort to hear people talk about Mama without bawling. Their strength was contagious.

Dear Journal,

Mathia's visit has spun me into a nostalgic mood. It's not a sad mood, though.

I'll always miss my mother, but I can't spend the rest of my days crying. Mama wouldn't want me to feel sad. I know she'd want me to remember the good times we shared. I need to build a life of my own. I need to have fun like a normal kid and dream of my future.

Salome isn't a baby anymore. She needs a strong sister, not a sniveling mess. I want to be ready when she asks the hard questions someday, too. I hope by then she'll understand that she can lean on me, as long as she doesn't lean too hard. I look forward to the day when she realizes that although I'm not her mama, I am a sister who cares for her almost as a mother would. *Guide my steps, Lord. Strengthen me in all the weak places.*

I made a bed for Mathia, between us girls. (I'd tried convincing her to sleep upstairs under the stars, but she wanted to sleep down here by us.) Salome played it for all it was worth and talked Mathia into weaving not one, but three stories. When it came time to sing our special good-night song, Salome made a face. "I want Mathia to sing. She sings better!"

Fine. Whatever. I'm tired of that stupid song anyway.

I think Mathia is going to be staying with us for a while longer. I overheard her asking Papa if she could stick around for a couple of weeks. He's no fool; he'd do anything for a change of dinner menus around here. And I'm the first to admit that I'd give anything for some help with the cooking and cleaning. It sounds like a perfect setup to me.

Dear Journal,

I awoke from a deep sleep, to strange sounds coming from the kitchen. Mathia was puttering around in her nightclothes, preparing breakfast. "Why would anyone want to get up this early?" I mumbled. I opened the front door to prove my point. Cold air whooshed inside like a conniving intruder. "See? It's still dark, Mathia. You're the only person in Jericho who's cooking breakfast before dawn."

"Nonsense! This is the best time of the day." Mathia's answer was plain and simple, like her appearance. She wore her hair pulled back from her face in a tight knot and her loose-fitting clothes in a neutral beige tone. She might not be pretty by most people's standards, but I think her bubbly personality is beautiful. When God created Mathia, he must have double-dipped her in a vat of kindness. I can see why she and Mama were such close cousin-friends.

Mathia's voice tugged me out of my sleepy haze. She reached over to inspect my delicate gold necklace, which I rarely took off anymore. "Deborah, it's lovely."

I slid my fingers under the cool gold chain. "Thanks. I guess you could say it's a family heirloom. Grandma passed it down to Mama on her twelfth birthday, and Mama passed it on to me."

"I remember when your mama used to wear it." Mathia elbowed me and whispered, "Want to hear a deep, dark secret? I was so envious of that necklace, I stole it from her one day and stashed it in a secret place."

Mama's favorite cousin—a common thief? I guess we all have "weak places" that need fixing.

"You took her necklace? Why? How?"

Mathia cringed. "Oh, I was a sneaky kid with a rotten disposition, that's why. I'd had my eye on that necklace, but I knew it was destined to go to the oldest cousin—your mother—not me. Eritha made the careless mistake of leaving it on the edge of her bed one day. I figured if she was that careless, she probably wouldn't miss it."

Mathia went on to describe how Mama showed up, looking for the missing chain. "I jammed my hands in my pockets and thought sure she'd notice my heart thudding against my gown," said Mathia. "I held on so tight to that dainty chain, I thought my fingers would never unbend again."

Mathia held me captive by her story. "As soon as your mother left the room, I dropped the necklace in my pocket. The rest is history." Mathia shook her head. "Pretty stupid, going to all that trouble for a little gold chain, huh?"

I gasped dramatically and pretended I was going to faint. "I'm shocked! Appalled!"

"But wait," said Mathia, "I need to tell the rest of the story. "I felt so guilty, I couldn't face my parents or grandparents.

I couldn't look your mom in the eye without a gnawing feeling in the pit of my stomach. I had no choice; I knew I'd have to smuggle it back into her room. So a few hours later, that's exactly what I did. I laid it on the edge of her bed, exactly as I'd found it. I don't think she ever realized it was gone."

"I had no idea my little necklace had such a colorful past," I said with a laugh. "Do you have any more secrets?"

Mathia acted like she was making a list. "Of course! But we don't have time to discuss them all today."

"How long can you stay?" I asked.

Mathia didn't hesitate. "Somewhere between a week and forever."

That's fine by me. Freedom, here I come!

A Question for Papa

Dear Journal,

I helped Papa light our lamps this evening and thought instantly of Anna. "Papa, can you do me a favor?" I asked. "If you can't do it, just say no. I'll understand." (That kind of approach usually captures either my father's attention or his sympathy. This time it captured both.)

With Papa's hectic schedule, I doubted whether he'd have time to begin a new project. It was worth a try, anyway. "Could you make a new lamp for my friend Anna? It doesn't have to be anything fancy."

"Why? What's the occasion?" he asked.

"No special occasion. They just can't afford a new lamp, and the ones they have now are junky. One has a huge crack and the other is so ancient, they're afraid to light it. It's almost as ancient as you, Papa."

"Well, thanks a lot!" he mumbled in his most ancient-sounding voice.

Papa ran his fingers through his beard. *He only plays with his beard when he's trying to find a polite way to say no.* "So, how are they managing without a lamp, anyway?"

Salome wrinkled her nose at her memory of Anna's house. "It's spooky and dark! And it stinks really, really bad, Papady!"

"That's an understatement. Papa, their walls are actually peeling and moldy. Disgusting! The smell itches my throat and makes me cough. Anna says they depend on moonlight and sunshine to give them enough light. Oh, and that's not all. Some tax collector guy has been harassing them for more money. Anna's mother says he's a liar and a cheat, but the Roman officials let him charge people whatever he wants."

Papa shook his head like he'd heard it all before. "Our officials allow those tax collectors free reign. Look at Zacchaeus—he raises his tax rate anytime he feels like it and doesn't have to answer to anyone. It's highway robbery!"

"That's the one, Papa," I said. "Zacchaeus. Anna says he's cold-hearted. Her parents are afraid he'll come back to collect more money. If they can't afford to pay those outrageous taxes, how will they ever be able to buy new lamps?"

I searched Papa's face for an answer. "So Papa, what do you think? Could you make a lamp for them?" I asked again.

"I don't have a problem making a new lamp, Deborah. In fact, I'd be happy to. I don't want to step on their toes, though—you know, insult their pride."

"But Papa, your pottery is beautiful! Why would a nice new lamp offend anyone?"

Mathia reached for my arm. "How long have you known Anna?"

"Only a few days," I said.

"And her parents—do you know how they'd feel about accepting such an important gift from a total stranger? Some people don't want help, Deborah. They'd rather keep their problems private, within the family."

Papa agreed with Mathia. "People have their pride, honey.

Anna's papa needs to know he's taking care of his family. How do you think he'd feel if you suddenly showed up with a new lamp? He might think the whole neighborhood was gossiping about him."

That's ridiculous! I'm not gossiping about them. I just want to help. My idea seemed perfect, but the last thing I wanted was for our gift to insult him. I was still thinking about it when I crawled into bed later. *I feel sorry for Anna's family, Lord. They're poorer than poor, but they don't seem to notice. The weirdest part is that they seem so happy! Would you show me what to do? I would rather lose Anna's friendship than embarrass her or her family.*

Dear Journal,

I sat by Mathia and Salome at synagogue today. Every now and then, I'd steal a glance over at Papa, who sat in a special section reserved for the men and boys. (I don't understand why we can't all sit together.)

Salome kept squirming like she'd swallowed a worm. Every few minutes she'd whine, "When is this gonna be over? I wanna go home!"

"Shhh-hh! Quiet! We're in God's house," I whispered.

She didn't care whose "house" it was; all she wanted was to get out of there and play. I whispered a bribe in her ear—a promise of a special treat if she'd be good—and she settled down momentarily. Then she spotted Anna's brother Nathan sitting on the other side with his father.

"Oh, looky!" she hollered. "Looky, there's Nathan! Hi, NAAAA-than!" Her screech startled a heavyset woman in front of us, who jumped so hard it woke her baby. By then, we had a howling baby and a screeching sister.

Little Nathan blushed at all the attention Salome was giving him and grinned like he'd earned some kind of an award. Papa frowned and threw me a *keep-Salome-quiet-or-else look*. Mathia reached across to shush Salome, to no avail. Salome was bound and determined to talk her new pal, Nathan. It was a synagogue service to remember.

Afterward, we gathered outside to visit with friends. Anna's family had crossed the road and were already hurrying up the street toward home, probably too humiliated to face the crowd. We caught up with them, and I introduced Anna to Papa and Mathia.

"Oh, I thought she was your mother," whispered Anna.

Anna's father kept a tight grip on Nathan's hand. He looked plenty perturbed about Salome's outburst back in the synagogue. Anna's mother was tight-lipped, too—not at all the chatty woman who welcomed me to their home. As for Nathan, he looked like he'd been stung by a wasp. He peeked around his mother and bellowed at Salome, "Don't talk to me anymore! I'm in trouble 'cause of you! It's all your fault!"

Salome stuck her tongue out at Nathan. "Is *not* my fault. Is not!"

He made a face back at her and mumbled something under his breath. Stubborn Salome wasn't about to give up. "Are you goin' to your stinky house? Deborah says it's too dark. And stinky. UGH!"

Lord, please just kill me right here and now, before I die of embarrassment!

Anna's mouth flew open. "Deborah? You said *that?*" She and her family kept walking and didn't look back.

I wanted to call after her—anything to erase the awkwardness of the moment, but my voice caught in my throat. "Salome!" I hissed. "That was a naughty thing to say, a very naughty thing! You should be ashamed. Apologize this instant!"

Papa scolded her, too. "It's not kind to say that about Nathan's house. How would you like someone telling you that your house stinks?"

"But my house doesn't stink. It smells yummy," said Salome.

Salome folded her arms across her chest and sulked. Salome and her big mouth! I'll never be invited back to Anna's house. I'll be forever labeled Sister of the Brat. I'm doomed.

Mathia read my sick expression. "Embarrassment isn't fatal, Deborah. It just feels like it at the moment." She gave me an affectionate squeeze. "Besides, I'm sure Anna's parents have more important things to worry about than Salome's 'stinky house' comment, don't you?"

"Salome needs a gag!" I said. "Anna's family probably thinks I'm looking down my nose at them. They wouldn't accept a new lamp from me even if it came with a year's supply of oil now."

"Oh, don't be ridiculous. You worry too much," said Mathia. "Give it time. Time fixes everything."

Mathia's words rang hollow. "Everything except for friendships and cracked lamps," I mumbled.

The sister in me wanted to scream. The substitute mama in me wanted to send Salome to a chair in the corner. And the daughter in me longed to lay my head on Mama's shoulder again.

Dear Journal,

Mathia shooed me upstairs at bedtime. I thought she might lecture me about pouting, but she didn't. "It's chilly tonight," she said, handing me an extra blanket, "but I think you could use some time alone." She asked if I wanted her to wake me early in the morning. "I'm going to buy some fruit and vegetables at the market first thing tomorrow. Want to tag along?"

"I'll think about it," I said. I'd much rather visit Keryn or Ziva. I'd like to see what's up with Anna, too, but was afraid I wouldn't receive a very warm welcome there, thanks to big-mouth Salome.

Sleep escaped me. The harder I tried to relax, the more alert I became. I watched wispy clouds slip between Jericho and the moon. Stars twinkle-peeked around clouds here and there, like tiny eyes winking "good-night."

Without moonlight, Anna's house must be pitch black tonight. Lord, please find them a lamp, I prayed.

I already have, God seemed to answer.

Between Friends

Dear Journal,

Jesus is coming to Jericho! Mathia overheard the news while she stuffed squash and onions into a shopping bag at the market this morning. "I've heard rumors like that for weeks," she said. "I guess we'll have to wait and see for ourselves."

Jesus travels a lot. He's already been spotted in surrounding areas. But Jericho? Why would someone like him want to want to dirty his feet in a place like this? Residents of Jericho have felt discouraged for a long time, thanks to the Romans' unfair taxation. Cheating tax collectors are getting rich at the expense of common, hardworking families like ours—and like Anna's. I heard Papa telling Mathia that our beloved city is becoming "a hotbed of dirty politics." He's heard talk that Zacchaeus may demand more money soon.

Uncle Yavin and Aunt Tara have actually seen Jesus in Jerusalem. "He speaks a lot about love and forgiveness," said Uncle Yavin. "It's easier said than done, though, especially with rascals like Zacchaeus."

I'm not sure how Mathia feels about Jesus. "All this talk of forgiving others who wrong you—it's quite a stretch, if you ask me,"

Bonnie Bruno

she said. She doesn't mind going to synagogue services with us, but try asking her a question about God and she'll throw up her hands. She acts like it's a big mystery, known only to the wise old rabbis.

Mama was just the opposite. From the time I was a little girl, I'd ask her questions. Most of them sounded like this:

"Mama, why did God make butter beans?"

"Why did God put spots on ladybugs?"

"Why does God live so far away?"

Salome would have loved Mama, because at three years old, she's now asking the same types of questions. My sister possesses a sweet innocence. She helps me to see things through the eyes of a child again, which is kind of fun. But the flip side is so frustrating! She bellows whatever's on her mind, like she did to Anna's family after our synagogue service. That's just Salome. She's curious and snoopy, and she says whatever pops into her head.

I wonder what she'll ask me when she eventually finds out that I'm not her mother. Sometimes I think she might already sense it. At Anna's house the other day, she kept asking about that "other lady"—Anna's mom.

I dread the day when Salome asks me the big question: What happened to my mama?

Dear Journal,

Well, it finally happened. Anna put me on the spot about my mother. She and her mother arrived at the marketplace just as Mathia, Salome, and I were leaving. Anna ran over to us and chatted away like she hadn't seen us in years. (I was relieved to find out that they hadn't held a grudge against us after Salome's big-mouth stunt at the synagogue.)

"So, when am I going to get to meet your mom?" asked Anna. "Every time I see you, you're with her."

Mathia smiled sweetly at Anna, but she waited for me to answer. My mind raced to grab the right words. How could I tell her with Salome standing there? Mathia understood my dilemma and pulled Salome aside. "Salome, honey, why don't we go on a little walk? I'd like you to meet somebody."

I rubbed my cold, clammy palms together. My mouth felt like it had grown a cotton lining. *Lord, give me words to help her understand.* "Anna, there's something you don't know about me. At least I don't think you know it yet."

"What—you mean about your mother?" Anna's big brown eyes seemed to see right into my heart. "Deborah, I already know what happened."

She couldn't possibly know. She hasn't lived here but a year. Mama left us three years ago. "What do you mean?"

"Your mother fell trying to chase down that old goat of yours, right? Is she okay?"

I laughed until I thoughts my ribs would crack. "Salome must have told Nathan about our famous goat chase," I said. "No, that wasn't my mother. It was me. Salome let Mikko out of her pen a few months ago, and I had to chase her down."

Papa thinks laughter is good for a person's soul. He likes to quote a scripture verse as proof. I agree; a long, hard laugh feels like a cool dip in the river. But every once in a while, I laugh so hard, it switches over to tears. That's what happened today.

I could tell that I'd totally confused Anna. "Deborah, I'm sorry! I didn't mean to make you cry. What's wrong?" She held my shoulders and tried to get me to look at her. "Please tell me."

I couldn't avoid it any longer. If Anna and I were going to be friends-good friends-she needed to know the truth. Secrets are safe between true friends.

So I told her about Mama.

She didn't shudder or act weird. She didn't ask a bunch of questions, either. Her response made me feel like I was being lifted up, up, up on soft, feathery wings. *Thank you, Lord. Thank you.*

Anna gave me a gentle hug right there in the middle of the busy marketplace and whispered, "I'm sorry. I had no idea. Deborah, you should have told me sooner."

That's all she said, but it was enough.

After I broke the news to Anna, we walked home together. Mathia and Salome trailed behind with Anna's mother. We parted in front of Anna's house, but not before I shared another piece of news. "Did you hear? Jesus is coming to Jericho!"

Anna seemed as excited as me about seeing this so-called miracle worker.

Dear Journal,

I slipped into Papa's workshop and sat beside him. "What are you making today?"

"I'm about to take a break. I completed a bowl this morning while you were away." He pointed to a fancy-edged fruit bowl sitting on a shelf behind him. "Who's the lucky person?" I asked.

"Think you can keep a secret?" He found my ear and whispered, "It's a thank-you gift for Mathia." Papa was as thoughtful as he was talented.

"She'll love it!" I said, running my finger over its smooth surface. "I'll fill it with fruit and nuts."

Papa seemed unusually relaxed. "What are you going to make next?" I asked.

"Nothing. Nothing at all. I'm going to watch *you* make something."

He dipped his hand in his water bucket and then reached into a deep container for a ball of damp clay. He dropped it on the heavy stone wheel and asked the question I'd been waiting to hear. "Want to give it a try?" he asked.

"Sure! I mean ... I think so. I don't know the first thing about making pottery, Papa."

I slid off the stool to stand next to my father. I'd been wishing for this moment for nearly forever! First I wet my hands and then cupped them around the ball of raw, wet clay. "I'll work the tread wheel this time," said Papa. "You focus on the clay."

The two of us made a good team. Papa pushed a foot pedal to control the spinning disk. The clay grew taller with each turn. I pressed my fingers gently around the sticky ball and watched it take shape. But within seconds, my creation spun wildly out of control. "Not so fast!" I yelled above the whir of the wheel. Higher and higher it grew, until it looked like a tall, skinny drinking glass. Papa let up on the pedal, and the wheel stopped abruptly. My masterpiece collapsed in a soggy heap.

"Why'd you do that?" I protested. "It was just starting to look like a vase!"

Papa grinned knowingly, like someone remembering his own first spin of the wheel. "Pottery-making takes time, Deborah, and lots of practice. If you're serious about learning, I can show you step by step. When would you like to begin?"

"Right now!"

Papa laughed at my enthusiasm. "How about tomorrow morning? Mathia will be here a few more days, and she can keep Salome busy during your lessons. Deal?"

I slapped Papa on the back. "It's a deal!" He didn't seem to mind my gooey, clay-caked fingerprints, either.

Dear Journal,

Mathia, Salome, and I slept in the upper room tonight. I warned Mathia about the risk of sleeping upstairs. "You won't ever want to sleep in the stuffy house again after tonight."

We laid there on our bedrolls side by side, Salome in the middle, counting the stars. "How come they don't all fall down?" asked Salome.

"They just don't," I told her.

"But why?"

"Because they don't. Now go to sleep."

"But how did they get up there?"

"God hung them, okay? Now settle down. It's late."

Salome moved close to me and curled into a tight ball. Within minutes, my little sister was asleep, steaming my shoulder with her warm breath.

Mathia whispered over to me, "Your mom and I used to beg our mother—your grandmother—to let us sleep upstairs, too, but Mama was afraid someone would tiptoe up the outer stairs and steal us away."

"I never think much about that. Mikko would go nuts if she heard an intruder," I whispered back. "She's an amazing guard goat."

Mathia told me stories about her childhood with Mama until both of us were tired. Mathia whispered the last words I remember before sleep overtook me: "Your mother would be so proud of you, Deborah."

Room for Change

Dear Journal,

I slipped out of bed long before Mathia opened her eyes. Our street was so quiet, I could hear carts clattering to market several blocks away. I would not be going anywhere today. Nope! Today I was taking my first pottery-making lesson from my father. I hoped he hadn't forgotten his offer.

The brick hearth felt warm enough for baking breakfast bread, thanks to Papa, who had risen early to get a head-start on his day. I flattened a piece of dough from yesterday's batch, which I'd left covered in a cool spot on the shelf. I liked making thin biscuit bread whenever I was in a hurry. Add a spot of fresh butter, a dab of jam, and breakfast was ready in a jiff. Papa doesn't think I eat enough, but who can stomach heavy foods first thing in the morning?

"I see my pottery partner is eager to get started this morning." Papa greeted me with a smile and paused to inspect my biscuit, which was rising into a delicious, flaky mound on the edge of the hearth.

"Don't get any ideas about my biscuit," I said. "You've already eaten breakfast."

We made our way to the workshop, being careful to slip out before Salome awoke. Mikko heard our footsteps on the path, though, and sounded a noisy alarm. Ori's two goats next door joined the frantic call. "I guess we won't have to ever worry about our house or shop getting robbed. Not with Mikko the Guard Goat around," I said.

My first lesson was fun! Here are some potter's rules I've made for myself:

1. Wear an apron! You would not believe how the clay flies around once the wheel starts turning.

2. Take a big chunk of clay (it's greenish gray—kind of disgusting looking, if you ask me) and squish the pockets of air out.

3. Plop it down in the middle of the wheel. Stand close enough to reach it without straining my back.

4. Step on the pedal lightly at first. Watch for flying lumps! Don't worry about my hair. I can wash the gunk out later.

5. Make a small hole in the middle of the ball of clay, almost to the bottom. Next comes the hard part—deciding what I want to make. (How do I know what I'm making until I think about it?) I stopped the wheel and thought for a long, long time. I decided to make a salad bowl.

6. Don't expect to do well the first time. I played around with my clay, mostly. Once I made the hole in the middle, I lightly pressed the sides with my hands. As the wheel spun, the bowl started to take shape. I accidentally made mine too tall. Papa says next time to concentrate on pulling down on the clay instead of up. That will make the edges of the bowl wider, not taller.

Afterward, I studied the result of my first lesson. "Not bad for a beginner," said Papa. I wasn't convinced. My creation looked lopsided and nicked around the edges. "A salad would seep out the sides," I decided.

"Sort of like me and you—nicked around the edges, but still usable," said Papa.

We washed our hands and hung up our dirty aprons. "Want to meet again tomorrow—same time, same place?"

I wouldn't miss it for anything. "Sure, Papa. But tomorrow I want to take my time and get it right."

"If you mess up, you can always correct it, honey," he said. "A potter needs to leave room for change. I can't tell you how many times I've scrapped a project and begun again." Papa chuckled to himself. "Sometimes I'm sure that our master Potter feels like scrapping me, too."

Papa has a way of twisting the ordinary, everyday stuff of life into a lesson. He can take a big fat blob of clay and transport a visitor all the way back to Creation. It's one of the special qualities Mama loved about him. One time she told him that he ought to make a sign for his shop, "Hiram the Storyspinner," and charge extra for sitting on the stool next to his wheel. "You could entertain customers while making their wares. You'd attract so much business, people would have to wait in line."

Dear Journal,

If today had been a color, it would have looked like an explosion of orange sparks. If it had been a scent, it would have smelled like a storm of lilac petals blowing across the Jericho plains. If it had been a noise, it would have sounded like a baby's first laugh. This was one of the best morning-til-night blocks of time that I recall having since Mama left us.

My very first pottery lesson didn't produce much to brag about, but I was happy about something else: Papa and I spent time together, just the two of us. No Salome interrupting with her questions and complaints. No busy project deadlines looming for Papa. No customers tapping at his door with new requests. Just

Papa and me, trying something new together.

Afterward, I helped Mathia clean the house. Salome dusted (we let her pretend she knew what she was doing) while I aired out the bedding. Mathia swept and picked up clutter Salome left behind in her morning play. Housework goes so much faster with Mathia here. I found myself daydreaming about what it would be like if she never had to leave.

"Come on, let's get some exercise and fresh air," said Mathia. We each grabbed one of Salome's hands and off we went. Spring was popping up everywhere, in bunches of wildflowers teasing the roadside. Birds screeched their warnings back and forth as we made our way past their nesting places. We had no destination and no special reason for our walk. We would let our feet decide when it was time to turn back.

Salome's feet were the first to protest. "I'm tired! My toes hurt!" she whined.

"We'll stop a while so you can rest," said Mathia.

I sprawled next to Salome on a grassy patch beneath a palm. A warm breeze lifted and dropped the giant fronds. "Look, Salome, they're waving at us." Salome giggled and waved back.

A trio of old women ambled by, all talking at once. "We'll need to leave early to get a good spot. No sense going if we can't even see him."

"This may be the only chance we have to see him in person. I wonder if he'll stop to talk."

"Oh, don't be silly!" said the woman in the middle. "Jesus isn't coming to chit-chat. He has more important things to do."

They bantered back and forth like schoolgirls, guessing as to whether the famous visitor would heal any local sick folks. "I wish my sister would come," said one. "She sometimes gets terrible headaches that last for days."

I strained to hear them as they made their way down the street and around the next corner. "Did you hear that?" I called over to Mathia. "Those women talked as if Jesus will be arriving soon. I don't want to miss it. Papa said he's going to invite Uncle Yavin and Aunt Tara, too."

"It's going to be the biggest event this side of Jerusalem," agreed Mathia.

Excitement rippled through me like the anticipation I feel before a trip. I could hardly wait to lay eyes on the man who has been assigned so many titles. But I wonder, who will Jesus say he is? Is he a prophet? A king? The Son of Jehovah, our God? Or is he just an ordinary man whose stories spread like flyaway seeds across the land? Did he really perform all those miracles we've heard about? It could all be true, or I suppose it could be one big fat lie, too. How will I know for sure?

Papa suggested that I should look into Jesus' eyes. "The eyes are a mirror to what's inside. They never lie."

Okay, so it's settled. We need to arrive early to find a spot right along the road, so I can get a good long look at those eyes.

Waiting for the Potter

Dear Journal,

Note for future reference: Never take a three-year-old on a walk without filling her stomach first. Halfway through our walk, Salome whined, "I'm so hungry. I need to eat. I need to eat NOW!" I told her she was out of luck, that I'd not brought the kitchen with us. I could almost see the wheels turning in her head as she changed her approach. "Ohhh-hh, my feet! They're going to fall off. Owie-owie-owie-OWIE!"

Mathia is a sucker for Salome's antics. She boosted her up onto her shoulders, which didn't do much to brighten the mood; it only turned a whiner into a louder whiner. Now, Mathia isn't young, and she certainly isn't fit for hauling the likes of Salome around. Her sweating face flushed, and I insisted that she put my grumbly sister down.

"If you faint, I'll have to roll you all the way home, Mathia. Here, let me take her."

I leaned down low so Salome could scramble up my back. She straddled my shoulders like a sleepy lamb, and by the time we arrived home, she felt like a dead weight pressing against the back of my head.

"It looks like your passenger needs a long nap," laughed Papa. He lowered sleeping Salome off my stiff shoulders and carried her into the house.

It might be fun to be three years old again for a day, to be carried away from problems and cares. I rubbed my hand across a gooey patch of hair where Salome had happily drooled her way home. *Never mind. Twelve is better than three any day.*

I followed Papa to his workshop. "Papa, guess what? People are saying that Jericho is going to have a special visitor soon. They're planning to line the streets to welcome him."

Papa didn't seem overly excited. "So I've heard. It's going to be crowded, Deborah, and you know how I hate crowds."

I hoped Papa wasn't saying what I thought he was saying. This might be the only chance I'll get to see Jesus, ever! If it means getting up hours before dawn, I still want to be there. I wonder if Anna's family was planning to go, too. One way or the other, I'll find a way there, even if it means going by myself.

Dear Journal,

Today's pottery-making lesson was the best ever. This afternoon, Papa declared that I've graduated to a new level. He says I don't squeeze the clay so hard anymore, like I'm afraid it'll get away. I've learned that if I want to make something tall like a glass or vase, I should lift up on the sides of the clay as the wheel turns. If I want something short and wide like a bowl, I need to pull the outer walls downward. It's as simple as that.

Papa put on a fakey orator's voice and waved his hands as though he were addressing a large crowd. "Ladies and gentlemen!

Boys and girls! I present to you a natural-born potter! My daughter, Deborah, destined for greatness." Sometimes he cracks me up. People call him the "quiet, creative type," but I know better. Papa is a comedian disguised as a potter.

I cupped my hands around a big, squishy ball of wet clay. "Watch," said Papa, curling his hands around mine. He pumped the foot pedal fast, then slower, then fast again. As the wheel turned, my ball of clay grew taller, then wider. When he took his foot off the pedal, I found an oval-shaped blob sitting before me on the flat stone wheel. "What is it?" I asked. It wasn't wide enough to be a serving bowl. It was much too short for a vase.

"Imagine a handle on one or both ends," he hinted.

I had a hunch but didn't want to be disappointed if I guessed wrong. "An oil lamp?" I asked gingerly.

Papa's eyes brightened. "Right!"

Next I learned how to smooth the rough outer edges of my lamp, by scraping a special tool across its damp surface. "Here, let's smooth the inside walls, too," said Papa. I placed my hands inside like paddles and pressed the pedal slowly. As the wheel turned, the inner walls of the lamp turned smooth and free of flaws.

Papa helped me form thick handles to attach at either end of the lamp. We reinforced the handles at the spot where they joined the main body of the lamp. Then he inspected my work inside and out. "Not bad for a beginner!" he said, patting me on the back. "I'm going to have to keep an eye on you or you'll be stealing my customers!"

I asked for a special favor. "Could I add something pretty around the top?"

Papa slid his new birthday toolbox over to me and let me sift through his tools. I found the curved tool Aunt Tara had given him. "I'll make roses around the rim!" I said.

The lamp turned out prettier than I expected. I left it on the drying table. When the clay has completely dried, Papa will fire it in his oven. I can't wait to light it for the very first time! I'll use it at night when I write my last journal entry each day.

Dear Journal,

Guess who showed up today? Aunt Tara! Uncle Yavin dropped her off on his way to a meeting with a fellow woodworker. She and Mathia gabbed so fast, I swear they stirred up dust. I could hardly get a word in edgewise.

Salome showed off and kept running her mouth, because Aunt Tara wasn't giving her all the attention for once. She kept talking about her spider bite as if it had happened just this morning. Talk about old news!

I'd like to pack Salome's bag and send her home with Aunt Tara for a couple of days. It would be so much fun to dive into more pottery projects! Papa was right when he predicted that I'd end up hooked on that wheel! When I'm working with clay, I forget the outside world. The wheel spins, but time seems to stand still.

I'm surprised that Mama didn't eventually join Papa in his pottery business. They could have made beautiful wares together. He learned from his parents—my grandparents—and has earned himself a good reputation all over our region. Ask anyone— they'll tell you he's the best!

Papa called you the Master Potter, Lord. Is it true that you fashioned me inside and out and made me different from anyone else in the whole world?

I've been daydreaming about all the pieces I'd make if I owned my own pottery shop. I can't expect Papa to turn over his wheel to me; he has orders to fill. If I had my very own wheel, though,

I'd make myself a brand-new set of dishes—plates, bowls, and serving platters. I'd make my bowls extra-deep, too, so soup wouldn't slosh on its way to the table.

If I owned a brand-new set of dishes, I would save Mama's set for extra-special occasions only. Every time Salome sits down to eat, I'm afraid she's going to chip another plate or drop another bowl like she did last week. Mama treasured her dishes, not because they were beautiful—they were boring and plain—but because they were part of our family history. Her parents had used them for years and then passed them on to Mama. Mama knew each plate like she knew her own thumbprint. Every crack, every chip stood for a certain event. *I'm chipped and cracked, too, but still going strong!*

Aunt Tara noticed the chipped platter after our meal together. "Look here, Deborah," she said, running her finger over the broken spot. "I was a little tyke, learning to wash dishes. I wanted to surprise my mother with my homemaking skills. Unfortunately, she wasn't impressed when I dropped a bowl on her best platter."

I helped Mathia and Aunt Tara clean up afterward. "These dishes are chipped and scarred, but I still like them," I said. I told them about my pottery lessons, and both of them praised me. Aunt Tara was especially impressed. "You're creative like your father," she said.

"And organized like your mother," added Mathia.

"Speaking of organization, have you heard the news? Jesus the Nazarene is coming to our fair city the day after tomorrow! Yavin has worked twice as fast this week to finish his projects so we can be there to greet him."

Mathia's eyes widened in anticipation. "It might be fun to see him. Jesus seems to attract a following wherever he goes."

I've heard stories about Jesus from some of the women around town. One older woman at our community well told the others waiting there, "He isn't like any person you've ever met. It's as if he shines a bright light into all the dark corners. Nothing escapes his notice. Nothing!"

My stomach triple-flipped. I felt torn about the possibility of meeting Jesus face-to-face. What if his gaze lands on me and he doesn't like what he finds? Will he ask me to change? Will he accept me as I am? It's going to be risky standing on the side of the road, waiting for the Master Potter to arrive.

I could always change my mind and stay home, couldn't I?

Parade Day!

Dear Journal,

Jesus is coming to Jericho tomorrow! Mathia helped me talk Papa into letting Anna come for a sleepover, but first she has to finish her chores. A clean room will up her chances of getting to come. Anna and I share the same problem: Today's clean room could quickly change into tomorrow's disaster.

Papa thinks I ignore Salome when friends are around, so I don't get many sleepovers here. I tried to explain that she's like a blood-sucking leech when my friends show up, but he wouldn't buy it. But thanks to some extra prodding from Mathia, Papa made an exception today. *Thank you, Mathia!*

"Tomorrow's going to be an unforgettable day, Hiram. Why not let Deborah and Anna share it?" Mathia was right. The whole town is buzzing about Jesus' visit. I just hope Jesus doesn't change his mind and pass us by!

Mathia broke the news that she's going to return home in a couple of days. She chased me out of the house this morning. "Go! Go! Enjoy your freedom while you can." The Leech followed me outside. "Look! Look! Somebody left me flowers, Deb'rah!" *Hmm-mm. Salome doesn't call me Mama much anymore.*

I caught a glimpse of movement and glanced up to see someone hustling around the corner—somebody whose head sported a familiar patch of shiny pink skin. (Salome calls it his "pink hat.") Ori stole a glance back at us before disappearing into his backyard.

"Hi, Ori!" I called over to him. "Look, someone left us a gorgeous bouquet from their garden!" I waved the bouquet high in the air where he could see it. "Isn't it beautiful?"

Ori stopped in his tracks. "Can't talk. I'm weeding," he called over his shoulder.

"Do you have any idea who keeps leaving us these flowers?" I asked. I whiffed the beautiful bouquet. "Mm! Mama would have loved them. She'd want to thank the person and tell him what a kind heart he has."

Ori dusted garden dirt off the front of his faded work tunic. He stumbled around for words and couldn't find any, so he excused himself and returned to his never-ending quest for weeds.

I burst into Papa's workshop. "Papa, it's Ori! We caught him sneaking away from our courtyard just now. Look what we found propped up next to the herb garden. It's the prettiest mystery bouquet ever."

I was arranging the flowers in our trusty old vase when Anna tapped on the door. "I'm freee-ee!" she said. "My parents said yes. I can spend the night!"

We took the stairs two at a time, with Salome hot on our trail. Mathia stepped in and snatched Salome off the stairs. "Come on, little one," she said. "Let's you and me find something fun to do."

Anna paced the room upstairs and stretched her head and shoulders over the retaining wall. "Awesome! You can see half the world from here! I wish my house had an upper room like this. I'd sleep there every night."

"Not if you had Salome ready to hurl herself off the wall," I said. I laughed at my next words before I even spit them out.

"And don't forget Nathan. Turn him loose in a room like this and he'd try to invent a way to leap from our roof over to the neighbor's backyard."

"You know my brother too well," laughed Anna. "Pretty scary, huh?"

Dear Journal,

Our rooftop sleeping area offered a perfect view of this morning's sunrise. I saw delicate pastel hints of dawn's approach long before it splattered Jericho's city wall with light. When the sun finally bobbed up over the horizon, I couldn't stay in bed any longer. "It's daybreak! C'mon, Anna, get up! We don't want to be late for the parade!"

Sleep played tug-o-war with Anna's voice. "I'd hardly call it a parade, Deborah," she croaked. She stared past the city's walls to the plains beyond. "Don't you wonder where Jesus is this very moment?"

"He's probably eating breakfast. Maybe he's thinking about us—it's possible, you know. They say he knows as much as God—including who will be at the parade today. Do you believe that?"

"It sounds almost impossible. Who could know everything about everybody?"

I raised my eyebrows like a teacher who is about to share an incredible fact. "God knows—at least that's what I think. And if it's true what they say—that Jesus is actually God's Son—then he also knows that you're still lazing around, trying to make the rest of us late. Get up!"

I could hear the family across the street loading their kids into a cart. The children argued back and forth while their parents tried to hush them. A donkey sauntered past with a bell around its neck, carrying an old couple dressed in their Sabbath best. Each passing minute brought more foot traffic, all headed toward Jericho's main street.

I pounded on the floor with my sandal. "Get up!" I shouted to everyone below. "It's parade day! Jesus isn't going to wait for stragglers!"

I waited for an answer. "Come on, you guys!" I called again. "If we don't leave soon, we'll miss the parade."

My sandals flip-flopped as I skipped downstairs. I half expected to find Mathia padding around the kitchen in her bare feet as usual. I thought Salome would surely be dressed and waiting impatiently by the door. One thing's for sure: I did not expect to find Papa lounging around the sitting area with his hair still uncombed. "Papa! Mathia! Salome!" I called impatiently. "If we don't hurry, Jesus is going to have come and gone before we get there. Come on!"

Aunt Tara and Uncle Yavin pulled up outside with their cart. "Time to quit talking and get moving. The early birds are here," said Papa.

Dear Journal,

I saw him! I saw Jesus today with my own two eyes!

See how huge I'm writing? I'm so wound up, I can't slow down. By the time everyone woke up, our house was filled with sunlight. Anna and I weren't hungry, so Mathia threw something together for her and Papa. Salome picked at her plate and stuffed a pear in her pocket. Finally, we could leave!

I guess I had envisioned us arriving before the main crowd showed up. But as we neared Jericho's main street, my heart sank. An endless throng of people streamed in from all directions. Older kids dashed across yards, looking for a shortcut. Toddlers skipped ahead of their parents or sat stubbornly on the side of the road, refusing to budge. Carts clattered by like they owned the roadway. It was a boisterous throng, bent on getting the best spot at the edge of the street.

"We'll be lucky if we can see anything with all these people in the way," grumbled Anna. "We should have brought a couple of tall stools."

I leaned against an old sycamore fig tree. Its bark scratched my arm, reminding me that I hadn't grown but two inches all year. A row of sycamores lined the road ahead—a shady invitation to hurry.

Salome's eyebrows fell into a frown. "I'm tired of walking. I want to see Che-Suss!"

"You mean *Jesus*," I giggled. "Jesus is coming to town."

"Je-sus," Salome repeated. "He's coming to see me!"

I blurted out my plan to Papa. He thought it was a great idea. "Go ahead, honey. We'll catch up." We ran ahead—Anna, Salome, and I—to the row of sycamores.

"Clasp your fingers together," I told Anna. I used her linked hands as a step to boost myself up into the tree. Anna helped Salome walk up the tree trunk and I pulled her up into the tree with me. Then Anna scrambled up to join us on a sturdy branch. "Lean back against the tree trunk like this, Salome. It's comfortable."

"I like it!" sang Salome. "It feels like a chair. A very tall chair!"

I surveyed the crowd from my spot up in the tree. I located Keryn and Ziva standing along the road with their families and threw a wave to them. Keryn nudged Ziva, and they both waved back. Suddenly I felt foolish up there in the tree like an overgrown child. If I'd been a nine-year-old boy, I might have felt different. *But I'm a twelve-year-old girl up a sycamore tree for all of*

Jericho to see! But it was too late to crawl down, not to mention too embarrassing. A tight group of people had gathered directly below. I was stuck up there now with a little sister who wouldn't shut up.

The Sycamore Surprise

Dear Journal,

The minutes seemed to drag on as we waited for Jesus' arrival. I could hardly stand the suspense. What would he look like? Would his band of friends come with him? What would I say if he spoke to me? How I hoped he'd stop at our tree!

"Maybe he stopped along the way to heal someone," I told Anna. "Papa said he's heard stories about a blind man from Jerusalem who can now see, thanks to Jesus."

Anna studied the crowd, which was growing restless and noisy. From my bird's-eye view, the crowd looked packed together like fish in a net. Every inch of space was taken, as they waited for the special guest to arrive.

I stretched to see around the row of trees and was surprised to discover someone crouched in the *V* of a tree next to ours. I nodded politely to the small-framed man, but he returned my greeting with an haughty smirk.

"He's little!" shouted Salome. "He's as little as me!" She made up a song about a "teeny-tiny man in a big tall tree."

"Hush, Salome!" I hissed. "That's not nice!"

I sneaked another peek at him when he wasn't looking. I'd

never seen a grown man that size. His flowing robe nearly touched his ankles, making him look like a boy playing dress up in his father's clothes.

"When do you think Jesus will be here?" I called over to him. He shifted uncomfortably and ignored my question.

"He's short in stature and short on words, too," I whispered to Anna. She hung on tight to a nearby branch and leaned forward to get a better look. "Deborah!" she said, clapping her hand over her mouth. I thought she was going to be sick. She lowered her voice and laid her head close to mine. Without looking up, she whispered, "Deborah! I think I'm going to faint! Do you know who that is?"

Her face blushed as red as last night's sunset. "That's the scoundrel I've been telling you about—the tax collector, Zacchaeus!"

"No way!" I whispered back. "He doesn't look anything like the cheating liar I've heard about. Look at him. He doesn't look like he could win an argument with a flea. How could an itty bitty guy like him toss his weight around and demand all that money from everyone?"

"It's him, Deborah. He's the one who threatened to throw Papa in jail if he didn't pay the extra taxes. Trust me, I've memorized his face."

I threw Zacchaeus a smug look and decided to not waste another word on him. How dare he show up to see someone like Jesus? "Well, that explains why he's hiding up a tree!" I said. "He's afraid to show his face in public, after the way he's robbed all those people down below. Maybe Jesus will tell him off!"

Salome kept tugging on my sleeve. "Who is that guy? He's tiny. Teeny-tiny! Teeny-teeny-tiny!"

"Now hush. And don't stare, Salome. It's not polite."

"If Jesus doesn't get here soon, I'm going to have a stiff neck," grumbled Anna.

"Shhh-hh, listen! Do you hear that?" I said. Way up the street, a ripple of cheers rolled through the crowd. Then we saw them— a band of men marching into town. Every so often, they'd pause so one person could speak to people along the way. *Jesus!* Children reached out to touch his hand. Adults pulled them back and apologized for their behavior. But Jesus didn't care. I saw him touch a child's cheek and speak to him, the way any father would.

Jesus! It's you! My heart pounded so hard, I thought the tax collector one tree over might hear its wild rhythm. Jesus worked his way down the street, greeting families and pausing to bless children.

Jesus, look up! Look up here! How I hoped he would stop and glance up at us. I especially wanted him to greet Salome. Surely Jesus knew about her loss—that she never had a chance to look into the eyes of her own mother. Those closest to the road strained to touch him, as if a simple touch was all they needed to make their journey worthwhile. I wanted that same touch for Salome— and for me.

As he grew closer, I thought of scrambling down the tree. I felt like a silly little idiot dangling up there above the road. Something made him stop to gaze up our tree. I saw kind, gentle eyes that seemed familiar, almost as if we'd met before. I waved down to him and he waved back, but words wouldn't come. It was as if my lips were sealed up tight.

"Is that Che-sus?" asked Salome.

"Yes, it's him. Isn't he wonderful?" I felt like I could float all the way home.

Jesus continued on. *Come back! Come back, Jesus, and we'll talk! I'll tell you all about my mama and how she left us too soon. Come back—please?* He turned back one last time and smiled.

But Jesus did not backtrack. Instead, he stopped one tree away and peered all the way up that skinny tree trunk. "Zacchaeus, come down!" he called.

"What? He's talking to that sleazy, slimy, tax-collecting thief?" Anna was not happy, not happy at all! We heard Jesus telling Zacchaeus that he wanted to visit his house today. *What?* He's going to sit down as a guest of the most-despised person in all of Jericho? What has the world come to?

Jesus, who supposedly knew everything about everybody, didn't seem to know a thing about this tiny man crouched in the sycamore tree. If he knew what that peculiar little man was really like, he would have kept on walking. I would have gladly set him straight if he'd asked. I'd have told him everything he wanted to know about Zacchaeus.

Anna hung her head, and I saw a tear slip down her cheek. "Why didn't he ask to visit *my* house?" she said. "Zacchaeus has stolen from hard-working families to pad his own fortune. And now he's getting rewarded with a visit from Jesus? It's not fair!"

What about me, Jesus? Why won't you come to my house, instead?

Dear Journal,

The crowd broke up a few minutes later. This time I didn't hear happy laughter and friends greeting each other. Many trudged up the road with heavy hearts. Others embraced each other and spoke softly in disappointing tones. Neighbors were outraged that Jesus was planning a visit to—of all places—the house of a dirty tax collector!

"He'd better watch where he steps," said Anna. "That wicked tax collector's floor is tiled with stolen money—our money!"

Salome didn't know what the uproar was about. All she knew was that Jesus smiled at her as he passed by. And that was enough.

Anna and I parted ways at the end of our street. She disappeared into her darkened house, and I continued on behind Papa, Mathia, Uncle Yavin, and Aunt Tara. Everyone seemed lost in their own frustrated thoughts.

Dear Journal,

Salome pushed her bed right up against mine tonight. We lay there talking about animals and make-believe story characters and friendly old goats like Mikko, until the horizon pulled the shades down on Jericho. Salome laid her chubby arm across my shoulder and patted me affectionately. Sleep slipped over me like a soft, filmy blanket and wrapped me up for the night.

Morning arrived not by way of sunlight, but by Aunt Tara's voice calling out across a shadowy room. "Deborah! We're leaving, honey. Wake up." She shook my shoulder gently. "Your uncle needs to deliver a wood project to a customer this afternoon. We're getting an early start." Next to her stood Mathia, dressed like she was heading to an important gathering. "I'm leaving too," she whispered. She leaned down to peck my cheek.

"Mathia, you can't go!" I said, holding her wrist in a tight lock. "You have to teach me how to cook that curry stuff."

She pried my fingers loose and laughed. "There'll be other times, I promise. First you need to focus on your pottery lessons. Your father says you're a natural-born potter. I think he's right!"

I stood in the courtyard with Papa, waving goodbye to our houseguests. "Don't stay away for long," I called. Uncle Yavin helped Mathia into the cart, where she perched next to Aunt Tara for the trip home. She wore her hair loose, and for a split second I saw Mama riding away.

"Good people," said Papa. "Fine, fine people." The cart rattled along the road, pulled by a mule who looked like he'd rather be sleeping.

Papa rubbed his hands together to ward off the chill. "What do you say we have that last pottery lesson?"

"But Salome—what if she wakes up?"

"Stay right here," said Papa. "We're going to have today's lesson at the kitchen table."

Forever Changed

Dear Journal,

I've been floating on air since my pottery "lesson" this morning. Papa returned with a linen-wrapped package. "Today's lesson is about pottery, but you won't be making anything."

I unwound the cloth carefully, guessing at what could be inside. When I saw it, I couldn't squeeze a single word out. Papa had glazed and fired my lamp, and he now presented it to me like a graduation gift.

It might as well have been a precious, jewel-studded treasure. I turned it over to check my signature. There, in the middle of the base, I'd inscribed a fully bloomed rose. It wasn't my name, but I knew what it meant. If I make more pieces later on, I plan to sign each with a rose. Mama would have done the same, I think.

Papa hauled an old lamp stand down from the closet upstairs, one that belonged to my grandmother many years ago. I dusted it off and set it next to my bed. It's going to feel luxurious to have my very own lamp—like one of the rich kids in those winter homes on the west side!

A few minutes before darkness fell, I filled the lamp with olive oil. Papa lit it, and we both stood back to admire my creation. "Yes, I'd better keep an eye on my customers, or they'll be placing their orders with the potter's daughter instead of the potter!"

Dear Journal,

Anna sailed into the courtyard today and breathlessly blurted out some disturbing news. Her eyes were so wide, I thought they might pop out of their sockets. "Deborah! The tax collector is coming! Tell your father that we saw Zacchaeus banging on doors two streets over. He'll be heading our way in an hour or so."

"But it's still too soon to collect taxes, Anna. Wasn't he here just a few months ago?"

Anna kept one eye on the road, as if she expected him to round the corner any second. "He's double-taxing us, that's what! My parents aren't going to sit still and take it this time, though. We're leaving for the whole day."

"Well, Papa says you have to look a tax collector straight in the eye and not let him see you sweat. Running off and hiding is not going to solve your problem."

I wouldn't tell my father this, but I don't think a crook like Zacchaeus cares whether we sweat or not. I think he's selfish and cold-hearted and cares only that we fork over the money. I've heard stories that Zacchaeus has no qualms about turning a person over to the jail keeper. No money, no problem; just lock them up and throw away the key. That's his motto.

I rushed into Papa's shop without knocking. "Papa, you won't believe what's happening out there! We've got to get out of here fast before—"

"Hold on, you're sputtering all over yourself," said Papa. "Catch your breath, Deborah, and tell me what's going on."

Papa reacted exactly as I expected he would. He sat there unmoving for a few minutes and analyzed the news. Then he returned to his work. I wanted to shout, "I TOLD YOU THE TAX-MAN IS COMING, AND YOU JUST SIT THERE SPINNING THE POTTERY WHEEL? WHAT'S WRONG WITH YOU?"

"It'll be okay, honey," he said. "Don't worry."

Papa spent the day meeting with customers who stopped by to pay for their wares. Each visitor brought up the subject of Zacchaeus' meeting with Jesus. It was the talk of the town.

A faithful old customer growled, "What was Jesus thinking, meeting with that lying cheat? You'd think a miracle worker would know how the rest of us feel about the scoundrel!"

"You can tell a lot about a person by the friends he chooses," said another. "Anyone who chooses to cozy up to the likes of Zacchaeus is no friend of mine!"

When everyone had left, I slipped in to ask Papa a question. "Hey, what do you think about Jesus? Do you think he was wrong to visit Zacchaeus?"

Papa spun around to face me. "I'm not sure. What do you think?"

"Well, I think he maybe wanted to tell Zacchaeus what a louse he is. And he didn't want to embarrass him there in public. I wish I could have been a fly on Zacchaeus' wall," I said.

I waited all day for Zacchaeus to show up as Anna predicted, but he never did. The sky didn't fall and the earth didn't shake, either.

Salome and I walked to Anna's house, but nobody was home. Zacchaeus never came, and they wasted an entire day running from him.

Midwife Mary made her grand appearance to check up on us. She sneaked up while Papa and I were talking and pretended she hadn't heard a word. "May I come in, Hiram?" she sang. Midwife Mary has a bellow that would turn anybody timid. Salome hid behind my leg.

"Have you heard the news, Hiram? You'd better get ready to dig deep into your money pouch. Zacchaeus is circling the city with his outstretched hand. Again." She sighed so loud, I heard her nose whistle.

Salome giggled behind my leg. Midwife Mary ranted on and made faces that seemed humanly impossible. I reached back and squeezed Salome's soft little hand. "We've got chores to do," I said, winking a secret signal. We tumbled out of the shop giggling uncontrollably, until a familiar little man with piercing black eyes stopped us in our tracks. "Excuse me, miss. Is your father home?"

Zacchaeus!

"Papa!" I shrieked. "Papa, you have ... company!"

Midwife Mary shot out of the shop like somebody had lit a fire under her. She didn't even say goodbye, just flew across the courtyard holding her tunic up around her knees so she could run faster. I don't know which was weirder, Zacchaeus' unannounced visit or Midwife Mary's sudden retreat.

Time stood still. I waited in the house and tried to keep Salome busy. I thought the taxman would never leave.

When I finally heard movement outside, I peeked around the doorway and saw Papa and Zacchaeus slapping each other on the back. Papa walked Zacchaeus to the street, gave him a warm goodbye, and sent him on his way. I dashed to the workshop to check Papa's money jar—the one he keeps stashed under his workbench in a secret compartment. It was still in its place and loaded with money.

Dear Journal,

Salome settled into bed without an argument tonight. She fell asleep in the middle of her story. That was fine with me; I'd been waiting for a chance to talk to Papa. This was it.

"Tell me about Zacchaeus," I said. "What did he want? Did he make you pay more money?"

Papa looked like he was basking in the afterglow of a miracle. "No. Zacchaeus has changed drastically, Deborah. The Zacchaeus you saw me laughing with is not the man who stomped in here demanding money last time."

Zacchaeus—changed? He must have tricked Papa good this time!

"He didn't demand any money. He didn't try to belittle or threaten me. He apologized! Can you imagine that, honey? Zacchaeus the ornery tax collector apologized! It's true!"

"I don't trust him, Papa! He must be up to something. I'll bet he plans to—"

Papa shook his head. "Believe me, Deborah. I was as disgusted as the next man about Zacchaeus' dishonesty. But he claims he's forever changed. He met Jesus face to face, and although I can't explain it, he says he has been transformed. It's almost like God scooped out the old Zacchaeus and replaced him with someone clean and honest—brand-new."

Papa doesn't usually jump to conclusions unless he's totally convinced something is true. I trusted his judgment, but I still had a nagging question. "Maybe he's different now, but how do we know he won't return to his old habits? What if he charges in here two months from now like the mean old Zacchaeus and threatens you again?"

"He won't." Papa pulled a covered container off the top shelf in the kitchen. "Look, honey. Zacchaeus paid me back all the extra taxes he demanded from us—not just the amount I turned over to him, but *four times* what he stole. He's going door-to-door, repaying everyone he wronged."

Lord, is it true? Did Jesus touch this scoundrel and cause such a change in him? If Zacchaeus can change, anybody can change!

Bonnie Bruno

A Gift of Light

Dear Journal,

I couldn't sit still. I felt like racing up the stairs and shouting my news from the rooftop to all the citizens of Jericho. Jesus had visited us but for a short while, but his presence would forever leave an imprint.

Ori waved to me from his garden. *He probably wonders where I'm rushing to at this hour.* On a ledge somewhere, a single bird serenaded my steps. It sang as if I were the only person in the world this morning. And that's exactly how I felt.

I reached Anna's house in record time and banged on the battered front door until her mother answered. "Deborah? Is something wrong, dear?" She invited me in and offered me a seat.

Daylight hadn't found its way into the house yet, and I had to feel my way over to a chair. An all-too-familiar smell of mold stung my nose. My throat began to itch, and I fought the urge to cough. "I'll get Anna. We were up late last night and decided to sleep in this morning," said her mother.

I reached for her arm. "Please ... wait a second, okay? I need to tell you something first."

I described Zacchaeus' visit to my papa's workshop and how he had changed. "He even looks different, as if someone softened his mean, tense features. He and Papa even slapped each other on the back like childhood friends before they parted. And that's not all! Zacchaeus repaid us *four times* what he had stolen over the years. Four times!"

Anna's mother covered her mouth and began to cry. She cried until I felt almost guilty about disrupting her morning. Maybe I should have waited and let her discover the news about Zacchaeus herself. "I didn't mean to make you cry," I said, patting her hand. "I just thought—"

"No, no, it's alright, really. I'm overwhelmed, that's all. I was so angry after news reached us that Jesus had chosen to visit that good-for-nothing Zacchaeus, I told my husband I needed to get away. I would have been perfectly happy to have stayed away forever."

Anna wandered out, rubbing sleep from her eyes. "Hey, Deborah. What's going on?" She glanced from her teary-eyed mother to me, then back to her mother again. "Mama, are you okay?"

I told Anna all about Zacchaeus, but she reacted the same way I had earlier. "I'll believe it when I see it. He's sleazy and evil, and he deserves to rot in jail! Besides, it would take a lot more than a visit from Jesus to change someone like him!"

"I know how you feel, really I do," I said. "Zacchaeus has hurt your family. He's hurt all of us! He'll be stopping by your house later today, and you can decide for yourself."

I'd almost forgotten the other reason for my visit. I pressed my surprise package into Anna's hands. "Here, I brought you something. Be careful, it's kind of fragile. And don't turn it over, there's something inside that will spill out."

Anna's brown eyes sparkled as she untied the blue ribbon. She unwrapped the soft cloth, pausing to peek under the last fold. She reminded me of Salome unwrapping a birthday present—slower than a snail, enjoying every second. "Deborah!" she gasped. "What have you done? Mama, look—a lamp!"

I wish I could have preserved the moment forever. It was just a dumb lamp, not a treasure. You'd have thought I'd given her a golden lamp studded with fine jewels.

"It's a little lopsided, and I didn't make the bottom exactly level. But Papa checked it over and says it should work fine."

"And you filled it with oil! We can use it tonight!"

Anna lifted the lamp over her head to look at the bottom. "Oh look—a rose! How'd you know I love roses?" She ran her fingers over the smooth surface and admired the nice deep basin. "It's so pretty, I'm surprised you didn't decide to keep it yourself."

"I was going to," I admitted. "Then I saw your dark windows from my rooftop, and it didn't seem fair. We already have three lamps. Why do I need a fourth? But the real reason I wanted you to have it is because I like being friends with you, Anna. I knew the day Salome and Nathan ran off that we'd become good friends, and I was right!"

"What a beautiful gift of light." Anna's mother spoke the words slow and sweet. "It's lovely, Deborah. How very thoughtful of you. You've given Anna something she's desperately needed for a long, long time."

A gift of light. I wonder if Zacchaeus feels the same about his visit from Jesus?

Dear Journal,

I felt light-footed and unexplainably happy on my short walk back home. I suppose some days are just like that. If this morning were like a plant, I'd scatter its seeds across the hills and plains until the entire countryside blossomed with contentment.

Bonnie Bruno

Papa was waiting at the door when I reached home. "Close your eyes. I have to show you something." He led me into the house, across the open courtyard to the kitchen, checking every few steps to make sure I wasn't peeking. He didn't speak again until we stopped. "Okay, open them."

A pretty, flower-filled vase sat in the middle of the table—the same vase I had admired in his workshop that day. "It's all yours, honey." His voice trembled with emotion.

"This vase was ... *is* ... special to me. It was the first piece of a dish set I'd planned to make for your mother someday. I know it's not the prettiest vase in the world, but I knew you had your eye on it."

I stared dumbfounded, unsure how to express my thanks. "All I care about is that it was Mama's. And now it belongs to me. Thank you, Papa."

We hugged as if we'd been separated for years. Then he held me at arm's length. "Your mother insisted on a simple vase. She asked me to not add any extra touches. She thought it would look more elegant without a trim." He paused as if he were reliving their conversation. "So I followed her instructions exactly and finished by signing the bottom with our initials."

My hunch had been right. *E* for Eritha. *H* for Hiram—my parents' names entwined forever on the bottom of an unglazed vase.

"Wait, there's more." Papa pulled a small piece of broken pottery from his apron pocket and set it by the vase. A handwritten message, scrawled in charcoal, read, "Remember me always." A wreath of wild roses circled the three words like a protective fence.

"Your mother adored this vase. When you were Salome's age, she'd take you on walks and return with huge wildflower bouquets. He dabbed at his eyes with a handkerchief. "I promised her that this was only the beginning; someday I'd make her a complete set of matching dishes." *Someday. How I hate that word.*

"But why'd she write this message?" I asked. I turned the pot-sherd over in my hand. It had taken quite a beating in the back of his dusty shop.

"Oh, your mother knew that I meant well. She knew I had customers' orders to fill before I'd have time to make anything extra for her. So she left me this reminder propped against the vase there on the back table."

Papa's shoulders drooped. "She never got her dishes, but God did grant her wish. I *will* remember her always, and I know you will, too, Deborah. Moving on doesn't mean we've left her behind. It means that with God's help, we can begin again."

Sometimes silence is more precious than words. Neither of us said anything for several minutes.

"Papa?" I said, breaking the silence. "Could you teach me how to make a platter someday? Nothing fancy—just a nice big platter with wild roses around the rim?"

"*Someday* is too far away. Come with me; I know where there's a big ball of clay with your name on it."

Bonnie Bruno

Life Issue: **I want to be able to be rest in God.**

Spiritual Building Block: **Kindness**

**Do the following activities to
help increase your kindness level.**

Think About it:

People pass through our lives like city streets criss-crossing.
Some are open and friendly, ready to offer a smile whether
they know us or not. Others shrink back if we make eye
contact, as if we're after something they aren't able to give.
Have you ever ridden an elevator filled with people in a
hurry? Most riders will mind their own business and avoid
conversation. Maybe they're uncomfortable around strangers
or preoccupied with their own thoughts. Or maybe they
don't feel like talking simply because their exit is only a few
seconds away. A few seconds—sometimes that's all we
have to make a difference in someone's day.

If opportunities to show kindness were measured like the

stops on an elevator, the world would suffer from a shortage of compliments, spontaneous smiles, and simple acts of courtesy. If kindness were as fleeting as an elevator ride, the lonely would soon feel lonelier and the underprivileged more isolated.

The Bible encourages us to look for opportunities to show kindness and to do good to others. Colossians 3:12 (NIRV) reminds us: "You are God's chosen people. You are holy and dearly loved. So put on tender mercy and kindness as if they were your clothes." After all, isn't that how God treats us, too?

False kindness is as useless as a fountain without water. It rings hollow because it doesn't spring from the heart. God isn't fooled by phony acts of kindness. Proverbs 29:5 reads, "A man who only pretends to praise his neighbor is spreading a net to catch him by the feet." God searches our hearts and knows our motives. He's pleased when we extend the same kindness to everyone, regardless of their position in life. In his eyes, we're all valuable. Each of us receives equal doses of his lovingkindness. God doesn't play favorites, and neither should we.

Kindness isn't expensive. It doesn't require special equipment or a special degree. We don't need a license to distribute it or fresh batteries to make it function at its best. It's planted in our heart at birth and nudged along by special circumstances God places across our path. His timing is perfect, and his purpose in perfect synch. All he needs is someone willing to step out and do the work. Could that someone be you?

Talk About it:

Can you remember a time when you felt lower than a caterpillar on a scorching sidewalk? What stands out most in your memory—the depth of your despair or an act of kindness that helped lift you out of a discouraging situation?

Imagine yourself clinging to a life raft. Boaters cruise by, tossing friendly waves and greetings. A helicopter buzzes overhead with a message to "hang on." A jet skier tosses you a bottle of cool water with advice to be patient and wait for help to arrive. As darkness falls, a cold chill sets in. Where are all the people who wished you well by daylight?

Somewhere in your circle of friends is someone who may be experiencing a dark, lonely time in his or her life. And somewhere out there, among the strangers who criss-cross your life, is someone whose life is filled with turbulence and uncertainty. A simple smile or a gentle word could mean the difference between hope and despair.

Do you believe that? What do you plan to do about it?

Try it:

Are you a good communicator? How? Think of the people you feel most comfortable being around. How well do you know them—really? Do you know their greatest concerns? Heartaches? Goals? Do you know what makes them happy? Sad? Upset?

Make a list of kindnesses you could extend to a friend or relative this week. Remember that hearts are blessed by even the smallest thoughtful act. People on the receiving end of a kindness don't carry scales. They don't measure the impact scientifically.

Send a note or email to a friend you rarely see. They'll be surprised (maybe even thrilled) that you took time to think of them. Invite a friend to share a family event—a barbecue, campout, or trip to somewhere special. Take pictures and order extra copies to share with them. Write a note to the parents of a special friend, telling them what your friend means to you. Buy a balloon bouquet for no reason at all. Honor a friend by remembering a special event in their lives, other than a birthday.

Nothing lifts the spirits like an unexpected kindness. It's a gift that has the potential to sprout and grow for many years to come.

Benjamin's Secret Journal

If you thought *Deborah's Secret Journal* was great, wait until you read *Ben's Secret Journal.* But you don't have to wait at all— here's a sneak peak at this exciting adventure also releasing September 2004.

Secret Journals
of Bible-Time Kids

Benjamin's
Secret Journal

Bonnie Bruno

• SAMPLE CHAPTER •
VIEW FROM A LEAN-TO

Hey, Journal,

I was glad for some time to think on the walk home. My head was bursting with memories of the past two days. I felt like I had been split in half—first a fisherman, and then a shepherd. I was exhausted, and home sounded like a welcome change.

"Benjamin! Benjamin, look up here, at the top of the hill!" I heard Peter yell.

A quick survey of the hill turned up nothing but bushes, boulders, and tall grass bending in the breeze.

"Benjamin, up here, to your left!"

Peter stood on a boulder waving both arms. What in the world was he doing running around the hill country so early in the morning?

We met halfway up the hill. "Are you nuts?" I asked him. "What are you doing all the way out here by yourself at this hour?"

"I could ask you the same thing," said Peter. "Have you lost your mind? Well, maybe I should rephrase that. Have you lost what's left of your mind?"

"Very funny. Who made you a comedian?"

Peter waved his arm dramatically, like someone leading a tour. "This is my domain," he said dramatically. "Come on, I'll show you around."

"I don't have time," I protested. "Believe it or not, I'm trying to get home so I can get ready for school. I've been out fishing with my father. Well, sort of."

Peter held his nose. "That explains the smell," he said, rolling his eyes.

My clothes smelled dirty from sleeping near the sheep pen, but that was another story. I didn't need Peter blabbing my business in class, so I skipped the part about helping Timothy.

Peter motioned for me to follow. "You're going to love this," he said.

I trailed him to the top of the hill, to a clump of bushes. Behind the bushes sat a huge curved rock formation. "Hold your applause," said Peter. "You haven't seen anything yet."

He parted two bushes in front, then crawled under a raggedy cloth that hung from a branch overhead. "Welcome to my hideaway," he said, stepping inside.

"A fort!" I cried. "And look—you even have fresh air and light." Tiny holes in the ceiling let in streams of light and fresh air.

No wonder Peter was such a genius! If I had a hilltop hideaway like that, I'd be a whiz kid, too. The cave was quiet and peaceful, a perfect place to study. "How'd you discover this cave?"

Peter jammed his hands in the pockets of his robe. "It wasn't hard. I bet these hills have dozens of caves just like this."

Peter offered me a cool drink. He popped open the lid to a wooden bin and pulled out an apple. "Want a snack?" The place was fully furnished and would make a great place to land after school every day. Maybe he'll invite me back sometime soon.

I would have gladly stayed there all day, but I had to get home if I was going to make it to class on time. Mama was probably pacing by now. You'd think she'd be used to my sidetracked ways, but she claims it's a mother's right to worry.

I reached home in time to eat a few bites of breakfast before school. Lydia flew around the corner to greet me and bombarded me with one question after another. "How many fish did you catch, Benjy? Did you get seasick? Did the storm toss the boat around?" I thought she'd never shut up.

"No, I didn't get seasick, and no, I didn't catch fish."

She looked like someone had knocked the wind out of her. "Huh? No fish? Why not?"

She gave it some thought, then started over. "How many fishes did you catch, Benjy—*really?*"

"Zero," I said, circling my index finger and thumb into a big fat O.

"No, I mean it!" argued Lydia. "How many fishes did you catch?"

I held my hand up again. "Zero, Lydia. None. Absolutely, positively none. In fact, I didn't even *see* a fish the whole time I was there. The closest I got to the water was when the wind blew mist across my face. The water was too choppy," I explained, "so we had to take care of boring chores like mending nets."

Lydia made a face. "I don't ever want to be a boy. Not ever!"

"Relax, Lydia. That's one thing you don't have to worry about, I promise."

Mama poured water into a washing bowl. "Go ahead—it's yours if you'd like," said Mama. "Lydia and I can freshen up later."

I carried the bowl of hot water to my room, where I scrubbed away layers of grit and grime. Rabbi had excused me to go fishing with my papa; I didn't dare show up at school smelling like a sheep pen!

At breakfast, I mentioned Peter's cave to Mama.

"A fort! It sounds like every boy's dream," she said.

"He has so much stuff in it, it almost feels like a house," I said enviously. "And guess what? He said there are dozens more caves like his up in the hills."

"Well, don't get any ideas, Benjy. Most of them already have occupants—the four-legged kind." The thought made me shudder. Would a snarly beast of the hills return to reclaim Peter's cave someday?

The walk to school gave me more time to think. I'd only been away two days, yet it felt like weeks. I'd sampled a day in the life of a fisherman and come away disappointed. In fact, I doubted I would ever use the words "fun" and "fish" in the same sentence again. My night on the hillside with Timothy wasn't that memorable, either.

I thought of Timothy's advice. Maybe I do need to slow down and focus on one thing at a time. Today, that meant focusing on schoolwork.

Rabbi's plump face stretched into a grin when I marched into class. "Welcome back," he called. "I'm happy to see that our storm the other night didn't pick you up and carry you off. So, how was the fishing?"

"Great!" I said. I could feel a fish story coming on—a very big fish story. What would my friends think of me if I told them the truth—that I didn't even go near the water?

Everyone waited. The pressure was on. Who was I to disappoint them?

"I don't want to cut into your lesson time, Rabbi, Sir, but I will say this: By the end of the day, I was so exhausted, I curled up in my father's boat and fell asleep," I said. "That's where I woke up in the morning."

Let them reach their own conclusions, I figured.

Rabbi patted me on the back. "Wonderful, wonderful. We will look forward to hearing more about your trip some other time. Now, let's begin today's lesson, shall we?"

Rabbi must have taken pity on me, because he didn't call on me to recite—not even once. Tomorrow I would be prepared— a promise I made myself during my walk home. School will buy me enough time to decide what I want to do with the rest of my life. It's a big decision and every time I ponder it, my brain ends up in knots.

After class, Peter took off without me. "So, how did your fishing trip go—really?" he asked. He eyed me suspiciously like a doctor probing for a clue to an illness.

"Great. Well, not great, but good enough."

"And what, exactly, is 'good enough'?" said Peter. He slapped his hand over his mouth to hide a smirk.

"I learned a lot, alright?" Peter was getting on my nerves fast. "My father invited me to taste the life of a fisherman, but the best part was staying with my cousin, who's a shepherd. A night on the hill is no place for weaklings, Peter. The country-side is crawling with wild beasts that only come out after dark."

"Woo-hoo!" shouted Peter. "You must've gotten quite an education out in the smelly pasture, dodging sheep pies."

Peter's lucky I was in a good mood. He doesn't know how close I came to punching him. "Well, it's obvious you don't know anything about shepherding," I said. I explained a typi-cal day in the life of a shepherd. "It's not all starry skies and sit-around-the-fire, Peter."

Peter wasn't listening. His eyes had locked on a white-robed stranger who stood far off the road, in the center of a bustling crowd. Grabbing both my shoulders, Peter asked, "Benjamin, come up for air! Look—Do you have any idea who that is?"…

Who is coming down the road?
What is the fish story lesson?
Who will become a fisherman with Peter?

Find out what has happened when you read
Benjamin's Secret Journal.

Releasing September 2004.

Additional copies of this book are available
from your local bookstore.

———◆———

If you have enjoyed this book, or if it has impacted
your life, we would like to hear from you.

———◆———

Please contact us at:

Cook Communications Ministries

4050 Lee Vance View

Colorado Springs, CO 80918

Or by e-mail at cookministries.com

The Word at Work . . .

What would you do if you wanted to share God's love with children on the streets of your city? That's the dilemma David C. Cook faced in 1870s Chicago. His answer was to create literature that would capture children's hearts.

Out of those humble beginnings grew a worldwide ministry that has used literature to proclaim God's love and disciple generation after generation. Cook Communications Ministries is committed to personal discipleship—to helping people of all ages learn God's Word, embrace his salvation, walk in his ways, and minister in his name.

Opportunities—and Crisis

We live in a land of plenty—including plenty of Christian literature! But what about the rest of the world? Jesus commanded, "Go and make disciples of all nations" (Matt. 28:19) and we want to obey this commandment. But how does a publishing organization "go" into all the world?

There are five times as many Christians around the world as there are in North America. Christian workers in many of these countries have no more than a New Testament, or perhaps a single shared copy of the Bible, from which to learn and teach.

We are committed to sharing what God has given us with such Christians.

A vital part of Cook Communications Ministries is our international outreach, Cook Communications Ministries International (CCMI). Your purchase of this book, and of other books and Christian-growth products from Cook, enables CCMI to provide Bibles and Christian literature to people in more than 150 languages in 65 countries.

Cook Communications Ministries is a not-for-profit, self-supporting organization. Revenues from sales of our books, Bible curricula, and other church and home products not only fund our U.S. ministry, but also fund our CCMI ministry around the world. One hundred percent of donations to CCMI go to our international literature programs.

. . Around the World

CCMI reaches out internationally in three ways:

· Our premier International Christian Publishing Institute (ICPI) trains leaders from nationally led publishing houses around the world to develop evangelism and discipleship materials to transform lives in their countries.

· We provide literature for pastors, evangelists, and Christian workers in their national language. We provide study helps for pastors and lay leaders in many parts of the world, such as China, India, Cuba, Iran, and Vietnam.

· We reach people at risk—refugees, AIDS victims, street children, and famine victims—with God's Word. CCMI puts literature that shares the Good News into the hands of people at spiritual risk—people who might die before they hear the name of Jesus and are transformed by his love.

Word Power, God's Power

Faith Kidz, RiverOak, Honor, Life Journey, Victor, NexGen — every time you purchase a book produced by Cook Communications Ministries, you not only meet a vital personal need in your life or in the life of someone you love, but you're also a part of ministering to José in Colombia, Humberto in Chile, Gousa in India, or Lidiane in Brazil. You help make it possible for a pastor in China, a child in Peru, or a mother in West Africa to enjoy a life-changing book. And because you helped, children and adults around the world are learning God's Word and walking in his ways.

Thank you for your partnership in helping to disciple the world. May God bless you with the power of his Word in your life.

For more information about our international ministries, visit www.ccmi.org.